All the best, Jodi!

Kristi Holl

April 10, 1990

Cast a
Single Shadow

OTHER YEARLING BOOKS YOU WILL ENJOY:

YEARLING BOOKS/YOUNG YEARLINGS/YEARLING CLASSICS are designed especially to entertain and enlighten young people. Patricia Reilly Giff, consultant to this series, received the bachelor's degree from Marymount College. She holds the master's degree in history from St. John's University, and a Professional Diploma in Reading from Hofstra University. She was a teacher and reading consultant for many years, and is the author of numerous books for young readers.

For a complete listing of all Yearling titles, write to
Dell Readers Service, P.O. Box 1045,
South Holland, IL 60473.

CAST
A
SINGLE
SHADOW

by Kristi D. Holl

A Yearling Book

Published by
Dell Publishing
a division of
Bantam Doubleday Dell Publishing Group, Inc.
666 Fifth Avenue
New York, New York 10103

ISBN: 0-440-40222-0

Reprinted by arrangement with Macmillan Publishing, on behalf of Atheneum

Printed in the United States of America

October 1989

10 9 8 7 6 5 4 3 2 1

OPM

TO MY FOUR SHADOWS:
Matt, Jenny, Laurie and Jacqui

Contents

Cast a
Single Shadow

1

Beginning of a Nightmare

Tracy Nelson stood in front of her locker as though she were an ice sculpture. She stared with horror at the newspaper clipping taped to the door. The headline seemed to scream at her: LOCAL WOMAN ARRESTED IN JEWELRY THEFT. The story filled three full columns, and under the headline was a picture of a worried woman. Tracy could barely recognize her mother's face.

The newsprint blurred as Tracy clenched her teeth and, with shaking hands, ripped the clipping from her locker and shoved it deep into her pocket.

She scanned the school hall for the culprit, but saw no one. Any person in the building could have taped the clipping to her locker. Still shaking, she grabbed the books she needed for the weekend. Even as she picked up her *English for the Seventh Grade*, she knew she wouldn't be able to concentrate on her short story assignment.

She slammed the locker door and hurried down the hall of the Johnson County Consolidated School. Two years ago, going to a consolidated school had seemed strange, but Tracy had gotten used to a school that held grades one through eight.

Rounding the corner, Tracy heard her brother's voice. She always knew where to find Doug. He spent every spare minute at school in Mr. Cunningham's science room.

Tracy didn't like science much herself, but she'd joined Science Club with Doug that year. Actually, she'd wanted to join the school's Book Club. But Doug didn't want to, and she couldn't imagine joining a group alone.

Coming into the science room, she spotted Doug and the science teacher bent over a table. She pushed her reddish-brown bangs back from her forehead and hiccuped.

Her brother spun around. "Hi, Tracy." His own reddish-brown hair stood straight up in front, kept on end by his cowlick.

Tracy went to stand quietly beside Doug. Although they were twins, Doug stood four inches taller than she did. His lanky frame sometimes reminded her of a wooden puppet on a string.

Mr. Cunningham glanced briefly at Tracy. "I was telling Doug how sorry I am about your mother. If there's anything I can do to help Laura, I hope you'll let me know."

Tracy stared at her shoes. "Thanks. We will," she mumbled. Mr. Cunningham had dated her mother twice in the past month. Tracy had felt uncomfortable around him ever since. She simply didn't like the idea of her mother dating her science teacher.

In the awkward silence, Doug motioned to the table. "Mr. Cunningham was just showing me a science trick I could use for my parties."

Tracy's brother was always looking for new science tricks for his "magic" shows. Over a year ago, to earn some money, he'd begun entertaining at children's birthday parties.

"We'd better get to Granny's, Doug." Tracy lowered her voice to a whisper. "Mom's going to meet us there after seeing her lawyer."

Trudging down the hall, Tracy reached in her pocket for the crumpled newspaper clipping. All the fears she had pushed from her mind came flooding back. She pulled out the article and smoothed it flat.

"This is what I found taped to my locker door." Together Tracy and Doug examined the picture of their mother. Tracy read the words of the story aloud.

> Late Wednesday afternoon police arrested Mrs. Laura Nelson at her home here in Centerville. Mrs. Nelson is charged with the theft from Simms Jewelry Store on Monday.
>
> Mrs. Nelson was employed by Simms Jewelry Store, where she has worked for two years. Stolen from the store were three diamond rings valued at $800 each and an emerald necklace valued at approximately $1200.
>
> The investigation is continuing, according to Lieutenant John Haley of the Centerville Police Force.

Tracy tugged on Doug's arm. "This article says the police are still investigating, but I doubt it. If they were, would Mom have been arrested already?" Her voice rose to a wail.

Doug tied his light jacket around his skinny hips. "Since the police arrested Mom, I think they must be sure she did it."

"But they can't *prove* it." Tracy's heart thumped wildly in her chest. "They don't have any evidence."

"I know, but they think she had a good motive

and the opportunity. I bet they're still looking for the missing jewels, though." Doug's scraggly eyebrows drew together in a scowl. "They haven't left us much choice. We'll have to do a little detecting ourselves and find the real jewel thief. That's the only way we can clear Mom."

Tracy skidded to a stop. "Yeah, but what do we know about being detectives?"

Doug snorted in disgust. "How hard can it be? You're always reading those 'Trudy Jamison, Detective' books. If some *girl* can do it, so can I. With both hands tied behind my back."

Tracy nodded slowly in agreement. Alone, she knew she wouldn't have a chance of catching the real thief. But she had the greatest confidence in her twin brother.

Warm spring sunshine covered the twins as they proceeded along Centerville's short Main Street. They passed Tony's Barber Pole, the Ben Franklin dime store, and Barnard's Hardware and Plumbing.

Tracy glanced across the street at Simms Jewelry Store. "I can't believe that Mr. Simms told the police Mom took his dumb jewelry. He's known her for two years. Lots of people, even customers, could have stolen it."

"Mr. Simms said that the glass display cases are kept locked. Mom has the key." Doug shifted his books to his other hip. "Since the safe wasn't broken into, he says the necklace and rings must have been stolen from the glass case during the day."

"But Mom didn't notice the jewelry was missing until Tuesday morning—you know, when she took the jewelry out of the safe to put back in the display cases."

"She's the only witness, though, who says it was taken from the safe," Doug said. "It's her word against Mr. Simms's."

They walked in silence for a block. "You know, I saw that emerald necklace once after school," Tracy said. "Mom wasn't busy, so she let me try on different jewelry."

"Did it look like it was worth $1200?"

"It was pretty, but not that pretty." Tracy shook her head. "But then, I doubt that the thief swiped it because it was pretty."

"A kid in my gym class today said Mom plans to sell the jewelry." Doug's mouth set in a grim line. Ever since their dad had died two years before, finances had been tight. "Lots of people need money these days, not just us. The police will need lots more evidence than that."

Tracy hoped desperately that her brother was right. In silence they passed through Centerville's tiny business section. Several blocks from Simms were the new senior citizens' apartments, where their grandmother lived in apartment number three.

They paused at her back door. Taking a deep breath, Tracy tried to erase the worry from her face, then followed Doug into the kitchen.

"Hi, Granny," Tracy said, forcing a smile. "What are you making?" She peered into a large mixing bowl.

The lines around Granny's faded gray eyes crinkled into familiar patterns. "Thought you might want a snack. I'm trying a granola recipe I found in *Nutrition For Today* magazine."

Doug draped his arm around his grandmother's shoulders. "Aw, come on. I thought grandmas were supposed to bake cakes and cookies. How about some good old-fashioned junk food?"

Granny playfully slapped at his hand. "Sit down and have some. It's good for you." She paused as the smile faded from her face. "I talked to your mother this afternoon. She said she'd be over around suppertime. She wants to talk to you about something."

Tracy's granola lodged in her throat. She tried to sound matter-of-fact. "Do you know what Mom wants to talk to us about?"

Before Granny could answer, Tracy heard the door in the living room open. "Ella Mae? I finished repotting this geranium."

Doug bounded toward the living room. "Hi, Andy! Come on in the kitchen. We were just sitting down for one of Granny's *nutritious* snacks. Please eat some or it will last all week."

In the kitchen Granny quickly smoothed her long apron and patted her hair. Tracy observed her with mixed feelings. She wished that Doug hadn't invited Andrew Blackburn to join them.

Andrew lived in apartment seven and was in his late sixties. He ran errands for Granny, helped with her garden, and repotted her houseplants. Doug said Granny and Andrew were "cute" together. Tracy wasn't so sure.

Anyway, Andrew was nothing like her grandfather had been. Her grandfather had died six years ago, but Tracy remembered him clearly. She had often told him secrets that she could tell no one else.

Doug returned to the kitchen, Andrew shuffling behind him. Andrew's neat blue sweater and narrow black tie contrasted sharply with Tracy's memory of her grandfather. Whether driving a tractor or dressed to go to town, he had always worn striped bib overalls, a work shirt, and boots.

"Thank you for repotting the geranium, Andrew," Granny said primly. "It was getting rootbound."

Andrew nodded. "I'm glad to help you, Ella Mae. Anytime." He sat down at the table. "I noticed your flats of tomato seedlings look a little dry too. I'd be happy to water them for you."

Granny's apartment reminded Tracy of a greenhouse. Each window was filled with hanging plants and pots of flowers. Plants climbed up trellises and snaked around poles.

Andrew cleared his throat. "I want to tell you kids how sorry I am about your mother. I'm sure this mess will be cleared up soon."

"Thanks, Andy." Doug grabbed a handful of granola. "But I don't think we can count on that. So Tracy and I intend to solve the crime ourselves."

Granny swung around, worry creasing her thin face. "Now, Douglas, you leave the crime-solving to the police."

Tracy leaned over the table. "We can't, Granny. The police already think they have a case against Mom. They won't be looking for the real thief."

Andrew plucked at his tie. "How do you plan to go about your investigating?"

"We haven't exactly figured that part out yet," Doug said.

"Don't worry, though. We can manage all right by ourselves," Tracy added.

"I'm sure you can," Andrew replied. "But I was thinking. Maybe you should check around. Find out who else has a key to those glass display cases. Surely your mother isn't the only one with a key."

Doug's eyes opened wide. "Like who?"

"The owner must have a key," Andrew said. "Maybe even the night watchman. They could take the jewelry without being seen."

"Andrew!" Granny spoke sternly. "Don't you go encouraging these kids. This is dangerous business."

Tracy threw Doug a warning glance. She thought they'd better discuss this alone. There was no point in getting Granny all upset.

Tracy leaned back in her chair, lost in thought. Although Doug seemed calm about turning detective, the idea didn't thrill her one bit. She loved to read about detectives, but she had no desire to be one. However, that was beside the point now. She'd have to help Doug find the real thief, to keep her mother from going to jail.

Jail. The word filled Tracy with alarm. Jails were tiny and damp. She hated to think of her mother trapped in a dark cell. Tracy knew from experience the terror that filled such places.

2

Detectives
Nelson and Nelson

Tracy's sober thoughts were interrupted when the
kitchen door was kicked open. Her mother paused
inside the door and set down two large suitcases.
"Can I join the party?" she asked, puffing slightly.

Jumping up from the table, Tracy said, "Here,
Mom. Sit here."

She frowned with concern at her mother's ap-
pearance. Dark circles surrounded her eyes. She
seemed to wear her cheerful expression like a mask.

"Mom, what happened at the lawyer's office?"
Doug asked.

Tracy flashed her brother an annoyed look. She
wished Doug hadn't mentioned the lawyer right
away. Her mother needed time to rest.

"Well, actually it's good news," their mother replied. "Mr. Sandler says that my trial has already been scheduled. In two weeks."

"Two weeks!" Granny slopped some of the fruit juice she was pouring into cups. "Isn't that kind of soon?"

"I think so, but I'm still glad. It will all be over quicker that way." Tracy's mother smiled determinedly.

Granny carried the juice to the table. "That doesn't give Mr. Sandler much time," she pointed out. "Can he prepare your case that soon?"

"That's what I want to talk to the kids about. For the next two weeks I'll be terribly busy. Mr. Sandler wants to meet with me every day. Since I'm out on bail, there are things I can do to help."

"What about us?" Doug asked.

"I want you to stay with Granny. Go to school as usual."

Tracy shook her head. "But we want to be with you."

"I know, honey. I feel the same way, but I'll be in and out at odd hours, whenever Mr. Sandler needs me. I'll come here when I'm free." She rubbed her temples tiredly.

Tracy chewed her lip. She and Doug *did* want to do some investigating on their own. It would be easier out from under their mother's watchful eye.

Andrew's chair scraped the kitchen floor. "If you need anything, let me know," he said as he left by the kitchen door.

Doug carried his worn suitcase to the living room, where he'd sleep on Granny's fold-out couch. Tracy's mother lugged the other suitcase down the hall to the bedroom. Tracy would share her grandmother's hard double bed.

Tracy whispered to Granny. "How does Mom seem to you?"

"I think she's doing well under the circumstances," Granny said firmly. She rinsed the bowls and stacked them in the drainer. "Maybe having the trial soon is good. Your mother will be found innocent, then life will get back to normal."

"But would the police push for an early trial unless they were sure of convicting Mom?"

"Hush, now!" Granny glanced down the hallway. "Mr. Sandler is a smart lawyer. He'll show those bumbling policemen how wrong they are."

"I hope so." *But Doug and I had better nose around anyway*, Tracy added to herself, drying the bowls.

If it weren't for Doug, Tracy knew she wouldn't have the courage to investigate anything. She had no false ideas about her own bravery.

Doug had always been the brave twin. When they were little children, he was the first one up the rickety hayloft ladder, or first one down the dark cellar stairs. It had come to be a family joke. Her mother said she followed so close behind Doug that the two of them cast a single shadow.

Tracy turned at the sound of her mother's footsteps coming down the hall. "How long can you stay tonight?" she asked.

Her mother's shoulders sagged. "I think I'll go on home now. I'm bushed and just want to get to bed early," she said. "Since tomorrow's Saturday, I'll pick up you and Doug after lunch. Mr. Sandler wants to talk to you both."

Granny turned from the sink. "Why?"

Her mother slipped on her sweater. "I have no idea. He just wants them to come to his office."

After her mother left, Tracy went to unpack her suitcase. As she filled an empty drawer with clothing, thoughts of the trial churned in her mind. Only two weeks away! With school every day, she was afraid that wouldn't give her and Doug much time.

Tracy squirmed for hours that night trying to fall asleep. She knew what would happen to their mother if they couldn't find the real thief. Doug seemed confident of their success, but Tracy had plenty of doubts. So many of her brother's wild ideas had failed in the past. Finally, in exhaustion, she drifted off into a fitful sleep.

The next morning after breakfast, Tracy and Doug plotted their course. They decided the logical place to start was Simms Jewelry Store. Closing the apartment door, Tracy made sure her notebook and pencil were in her pocket. During the interview with Mr. Simms, Doug would ask questions while she recorded the answers.

In a few minutes they'd arrived downtown, and Doug marched directly to the Simms Jewelry Store. Tracy's heart beat like a trapped bird she had once seen. She squared her thin shoulders and followed her brother into the shop.

The chimes above the door played merrily as Tracy glanced around the store. Glass display cases were filled with jewelry: rings, necklaces, pendants, and bracelets. Rotating displays of watches turned smoothly.

Plush maroon carpeting muffled Tracy's and Doug's steps. A new clerk was busy showing a young couple some wedding rings. The only other customer was a man standing near the watch display. He looked like a mannequin in his neat gray three-piece suit and gray hat. Tracy would hardly have noticed him at all, except for one thing.

The man barely glanced at the watches. Although he stood motionless, his eyes darted back and forth. Tracy knew she was probably too suspicious, but she recorded the man's behavior in her notebook anyway.

At the back of the store, Mr. Simms sat at a large polished table. A ledger lay open in front of him. He rose slowly, with a frosty smile for Tracy and Doug.

"I'm surprised to see you two in the store. Is there something I can do for you?"

Doug shook hands with Mr. Simms, pulling himself up to his full five feet, four inches. "We'd like to ask you a few questions."

Tracy whipped open her notebook. Stepping behind Doug, she thought how much Mr. Simms's protruding eyes and green suit made him look like a frog. Did his tongue dart out when flies came near?

"Questions?" Mr. Simms's voice dripped icicles. "About what?"

"We're not satisfied with the police investigation into the thefts from your store." Doug's voice cracked, dropping from tenor to bass. "Our mother could never have done it, so there must be a thief running around free. We intend to find him."

"And how can I *possibly* help you with that?"

Doug motioned for Tracy to begin taking notes. "To start with, when were the stolen necklace and rings last seen?"

Mr. Simms shrugged. "The police asked that the first thing. I noticed the jewelry was missing Tuesday morning. It was time for your mother to put the jewelry in the display cases, as she does every morning."

Tracy spoke without thinking. "Then obviously the safe was broken into during the night!"

"I'm afraid not. There was no evidence that the safe had been tampered with." Mr. Simms shook his head firmly. "The jewelry must have been taken when your mother put it away Monday night. It would be a simple matter to slip it into a dress pocket."

"You take that back!" Doug burst out. His face turned a deep purple, making his freckles disappear. "Our mother's worked here almost two years. Why would she do that now?"

"Just last week, your mother came to me asking for a sizable raise. Business has been slow, and I had to refuse. Obviously she stole the jewelry to pawn for the money she needs."

"How do you know the jewelry was still there Monday?" Doug shouted. "There are *hundreds* of pieces of jewelry in this store. You can't possibly keep track of every one of them. The jewelry could have disappeared anytime."

Tracy nodded eagerly, admiring her brother's quick thinking.

Mr. Simms's bulging eyes narrowed. "I saw your mother trying on that emerald necklace Monday after lunch," he said. "She was modeling the necklace for Mr. Drake, one of our customers."

Suddenly Tracy remembered Andrew's suggestion. "Surely Mom didn't have the only key to the glass cases. Don't you have a key yourself? And don't you also know the combination to the safe?"

Mr. Simms's frog eyes looked ready to pop. "How dare you! Are you suggesting that I stole the jewelry from myself?" He lumbered over to Tracy, towering above her. "I think I've heard enough."

Tracy pivoted quickly and headed for the door. Doug fell into step beside her. "I'm sorry I made him mad," she whispered.

Doug shrugged. "We weren't getting much information from him anyway." He glanced over his shoulder. "Either he honestly believes Mom is guilty, or he's trying to blame her for some other reason." Doug motioned to her notebook. "Did you write down everything he said?"

"Sure did," Tracy said. "See?" She flipped it open to display several pages of dots in different patterns.

"Good idea!" Doug bent over the notebook, slowly deciphering her code. "Now no one can read these notes except you and me."

Tracy closed the notebook, pleased that Doug remembered. Last year each student in their class had had a pen pal from the state blind school. Ever since Tracy used Braille when making private notes.

She slipped the notebook back into her pocket. "Let's detour to Kids Korner on the way home," she said. "I need to see Mrs. Jenkins."

She and Doug turned and headed toward Mrs. Jenkins's day care center. Tracy worked after school two afternoons a week as a volunteer and loved it. After several months of working with the children, she'd decided she wanted to be a nursery school teacher one day.

Oddly enough, Kids Korner stood right in the middle of the block. A chain-link fence surrounded a backyard that was filled with teeter-totters, sandboxes, and swings. Twelve screeching children under the age of four raced around the yard.

Tracy spotted Mrs. Jenkins and waved to her as she unhooked the gate.

Doug stayed on the sidewalk. "Don't get busy

playing with the kids. It's almost noon. Mom is taking us to Mr. Sandler's office right after lunch, remember.''

Tracy nodded and closed the gate carefully behind her. "Hi, Mrs. Jenkins," she called. Several children wrapped themselves around Tracy's legs and begged her to push them on the swings.

"Hi, Tracy," Mrs. Jenkins said, looking strangely uncomfortable.

"I just stopped to see when you want me to come next week." Tracy's schedule varied from week to week.

Mrs. Jenkins rubbed her tennis shoe through the grass. "I hardly know how to say this, Tracy." Her mouth set in a grim line. "A few mothers are concerned about your working here. They don't think it's . . . wise."

"What's the problem?" Tracy asked, her throat tightening.

"I'm afraid it's the bad publicity about your mother," Mrs. Jenkins replied. "Maybe you should take a short vacation. As soon as your mother's found innocent, I'll be happy to have you back. I hope you understand."

Tracy nodded, forcing her lips into an unsteady smile. "Sure. I understand."

Stumbling back across the yard, she let herself out the gate. In halting sentences, she explained what had happened. "It's just between you and me," she warned Doug. "If Mom heard about it, she'd feel terrible, like it was her fault. I don't want her more upset than she already is."

They walked the rest of the way to Granny's in silence. After alfalfa sprout sandwiches, Tracy and Doug waited outside for their mother. Tracy couldn't imagine why Mr. Sandler wanted to see them.

It didn't take long to find out. At the lawyer's office, Mr. Sandler seated Tracy, Doug, and their mother in front of his desk. He drummed his fingers on the glass top and hummed.

Taking a deep breath, Mr. Sandler clasped his muscular fingers together. "I won't keep you in suspense. I want you kids to know where things stand. I talked to Lieutenant Haley today," he said briskly. "The truth is, the police have stopped hunting for any other suspects. They are convinced that they have enough evidence to convict your mother."

His words hung heavily in the still air. Tracy watched as her mother's face was slowly drained of all its color.

Doug leaned over the desk. "Andrew—a friend of Granny's—suggested that Mr. Simms or the night watchman or even a customer might be guilty. Why haven't the police thought of that?"

Mr. Sandler hunched his massive shoulders.

"Just between us, I think your mother was an easy person to pin the crime on. Mr. Simms is a wealthy man and has considerable influence in this community. The police felt pressured to find the thief quickly."

"So what are you going to do?" demanded Tracy.

"Oh, I have a few ideas up my sleeve," Mr. Sandler assured her. For the first time he smiled faintly. "Please understand if you don't see your mother much in the next two weeks. We can't leave any stone unturned."

Squirming in her padded chair, Tracy realized her mother hadn't said a word since entering the office. She merely stared out the second-story window. Finally she cleared her throat noisily. "I don't think your investigating will be necessary."

Tracy frowned, puzzled by her mother's stricken face. "What do you mean, Mom?"

"I hate to admit it," her mother said, taking a deep, shuddering breath, "but I think I know who took the jewelry."

3

Accident!

Tracy's mouth fell open in shock. She felt as if someone had smacked her hard between the shoulder blades. "Mom, what are you saying?" she demanded. "Who do you think the thief is?"

Saying nothing, Tracy's mother returned to staring out the window. Mr. Sandler sat like a massive stone statue.

Tracy shook her mother's arm. "Why haven't you said anything before now?"

As if coming out of a trance, Mr. Sandler blinked his eyes. "Sit down, Tracy. I'll get to the bottom of this." He rapped his knuckles on his desk. "Laura, I can't believe you've known who the thief is all along and haven't spoken up before."

Closing her eyes briefly, her mother's voice

sounded very small when she spoke. "I guess I should have said something, but I haven't been absolutely sure. I'm still not. I know how it feels to be unjustly accused of something. I don't want an innocent person to get hurt."

Mr. Sandler's eyes narrowed. "Who are you trying to protect?"

"There's a girl," Tracy's mother said slowly. "Her name is Lisa Curran, and she's only fourteen. After school she often comes in the store."

Tracy remembered Lisa from school—a quiet girl, always alone. "What makes you think Lisa stole the jewelry?" she asked, confused.

"She likes to try on jewelry," her mother explained. "She was in the store just before closing time Monday afternoon. Mr. Simms once told me she has a shoplifting record from an incident when she was thirteen."

Doug spoke for the first time. "Then you've been trying to protect her? You let the police arrest you and got your picture on the front page of the newspaper to protect a *stranger*?"

Tracy's mother clasped her hands together, her knuckles white and knobby. "I hated to point a finger at Lisa. I so hoped that if I kept quiet long enough, the police would find the criminal. I didn't want to believe Lisa had taken the jewelry."

Doug pushed his hair straight up in front. "Lisa's tried on jewelry in the past, but nothing's turned up missing before?"

"That's right. Lots of times." Her mother looked from Tracy to Doug. "But Monday when she was trying on rings and necklaces, I was called away from the counter for a phone call. Remember, Tracy, when you called to say you would be late?"

Tracy nodded. She and Sharon Littleton had volunteered to help the school librarian go through some boxes of donated books.

"When I returned from talking to you, Lisa had left. It was closing time, so I didn't think anything was strange. I helped Mr. Simms put the jewelry in the safe, then went home."

Mr. Sandler leaned forward eagerly. "Did you notice that the jewelry was missing then?"

"We were in a hurry, talking as we worked. I didn't notice anything missing until Tuesday morning when I put the jewelry back in the display cases. Then I remembered Lisa." She stared at Doug and Tracy. "But I don't want Lisa accused, not yet. *Please* understand. She's a troubled girl and being falsely accused could destroy her. She thinks of me as her friend."

Mr. Sandler folded his thick fingers together and nodded at Tracy and Doug. "I need to talk to your mother privately. Perhaps you'd like to go back to your grandmother's home."

Surprised at the abrupt dismissal, Tracy stood to leave with Doug. Outside the lawyer's office, she tried to breathe deeply. "What is going *on*?" she asked, sounding almost hysterical.

Doug frowned. "I don't know. But I don't believe Mom would protect someone she knew was guilty. She just has to be sure about Lisa."

"I just wish the police were still looking. *We* can't report Lisa, knowing how Mom feels about it." They started down the street. "But what do we do?"

Doug snapped his fingers. "We go back to the beginning. Only it's no more Mister Nice Guy. We're going to be ruthless in our investigation. We'll dig in places we'd rather not dig in and spy on people we'd rather not spy on. We have to do it for Mom. Agreed?"

"Agreed." Tracy gulped. She knew her Bravery Quotient was extremely low. "I'll be right behind you, taking careful notes."

Doug hiked down the street, and Tracy ran to keep up with his long strides. "We'll go back to Simms then. The janitor might have noticed things around the store the others missed."

Tracy trotted after him, checking her pocket for the notebook and pencil. She'd be ready. She only hoped they uncovered a clue important enough to write down.

Their steps slowed as they neared Simms Jewelry Store. Standing on the sidewalk with a bucket and a squeegee was a short, wiry man. Tracy watched him wash the store's large picture window, then wipe it dry with the squeegee.

Doug stepped forward. "Excuse me. Are you the janitor who works for Mr. Simms?"

The small man in the black t-shirt turned around. "Sure am. Bert Benson's the name," he said, leaning on the squeegee.

Doug nodded at Tracy. "We're Laura Nelson's kids. Could we ask you some questions?"

Tracy gripped her notebook and pencil with sweaty hands. She didn't like standing in front of the store's window. Mr. Simms could look out at any minute and spot them.

The janitor's smile helped her relax a little. "Ask away, but I don't know if I can help. I've only worked here six months."

"Do you know our mother?"

"Sure do. Nice woman. She once got me some handyman jobs around your grandmother's apartment building."

Doug's face brightened at the friendly words. "We know Mom didn't steal Mr. Simms's jewelry.

We're trying to find out who did," he said. "When do you work here?"

"I come on at four o'clock in the afternoon and work until eight o'clock."

Tracy wrote quickly in her notebook, the patterns of Braille dots filling half the page.

"Do you have a key to the building?" Doug asked. "Mom thinks the jewelry was stolen during the night while the building was locked."

Bert scratched his head. "No. Don't have a key. No need. Mr. Simms has a key. If he leaves before I get done cleaning, then Jake locks up."

"Jake?"

"Jake Woodsly. Night watchman. Worked here for years, I think. Stays on duty all night, until Mr. Simms comes to work in the morning."

Tracy wrote hurriedly, filling the page with dots. It sounded as if Andrew had been right. Mr. Simms and the night watchman had both had a chance to rob the safe.

Just then Mr. Simms threw open the front door. "I thought I told you kids to stay away from here!" he yelled. His bulging frog eyes nearly popped out of his face. "Go away and don't come back!"

Bert Benson shook his head slowly. "They were just asking me a few questions. No need to get excited."

Mr. Simms flushed a deeper shade of red. "Correct me if I'm wrong! I pay you to keep the store clean, *not* stand on the sidewalk chatting your time away. Now get to work or you're fired!"

Through stiff jaws, Bert answered. "Yes, sir. Sorry, sir."

Tracy noticed the janitor's fists clenched around the handle of the squeegee. She knew he was angry at Mr. Simms, and she didn't blame him one bit. Tracy stuck the notebook back in her pocket. "Thanks, Mr. Benson," she said.

"We'll be seeing you," Doug added, pulling Tracy after him down the sidewalk. Doug glanced over his shoulder every few seconds.

When Mr. Simms disappeared back into his store, they stopped. Thoughtfully Tracy watched Bert Benson polish the glass in the door. "Well, do you think we got anything?" she asked.

"Mr. Simms is either a real grouch, or he has something to hide," Doug said firmly. "Bert Benson seems innocent enough, but you can never tell about appearances."

Tracy shook her wrist. "My watch stopped. I don't know for sure, but I think it's getting late. Granny's probably wondering where we are."

"Let's go back and cut through the alley next to the jewelry store," Doug suggested. "We can get to Granny's in half the time."

They backtracked and started down the alley. After standing in the hot sun, Tracy welcomed the coolness of the shaded alley. Abruptly she stopped, grabbing Doug's sleeve. "Listen!" she whispered.

Voices drifted into the deserted alley from somewhere. Tracy poked Doug in the ribs and pointed up. A small window in a room over the jewelry store was open. The voice coming from the room definitely belonged to Mr. Simms.

Doug pointed to the fire escape underneath the window. He pantomimed climbing up the fire escape to listen at the window.

Tracy shook her head vigorously, but Doug ignored her and crept up the rusty fire escape. Hesitating for only an instant, Tracy followed him. They crouched at the top on the landing. Tracy's hand shook as she flipped open her notebook to a blank page.

"If that's all, Mr. Simms, I'll begin my rounds," said a strange voice near the window. A chair scraped the floor inside the room.

"Thanks, Jake," Mr. Simms answered. "I guess I've let business worry me too much lately. With money tight, people don't buy a lot of jewelry."

The man's voice moved away from the window. "I'll go now, Mr. Simms. If there's anything else you want, let me know."

"Sure will. I really appreciate what you've done. You'll find a little extra in your paycheck this week," Mr. Simms said.

Tracy leaned close to Doug's ear. "Did you hear that?" she whispered. "If business is so bad, why is Mr. Simms giving Jake extra money in his paycheck?"

"Maybe it's a pay-off. Maybe Jake took the jewelry at night, while Mr. Simms had an alibi. Then they pawned it. Mr. Simms could then collect on the insurance too," Doug whispered back.

Tracy's voice rose in her excitement. "That must be it!" Horrified, she clapped her hand over her mouth.

A shout came from inside the room. "Did you hear something? It sounded like voices out on the fire escape!"

Tracy gasped as Mr. Simms's angry face appeared at the window. She grabbed the hand rail and turned to flee down the fire escape.

"Hey, you! It's the Nelson kids!" Mr. Simms yelled.

Out of the corner of her eye Tracy saw sudden movement. Mr. Simms's arm shot out the window toward Doug. Doug spotted Mr. Simms's hand just in time and jumped back.

As if in slow motion, Tracy saw Doug's foot slip on the fire escape. He grabbed for the railing, but his hands clutched empty air. Falling over the railing backwards, he landed in the alley with a hollow thud.

No longer worried about making noise, Tracy clattered down the fire escape. "Doug! Doug! Are you all right?"

Doug groaned and opened his eyes. "It's my leg. It's killing me," he said, chewing his lower lip.

Tracy rolled up his pants leg. Halfway between his knee and ankle, a sharp bulge pushed against the skin. Tracy was afraid that a broken bone was close to the surface.

"Don't move, Doug. Just lie still," Tracy cautioned. She looked up and called to Mr. Simms who still hung out the window. "Call an ambulance! I think his leg's broken!"

Mr. Simms disappeared into the room, and Tracy heard him on the telephone. Within five minutes, the ambulance had arrived. Friendly but brisk, the two men asked Tracy to stand back while they worked. Soon they lifted Doug onto a stretcher and into the ambulance.

Tracy climbed in with them and the attendant slammed shut the back door. Tracy's last sight before the door closed was an angry Mr. Simms standing and watching. She shuddered at the menacing look on his face.

Tracy patted Doug's shoulder on the way to the hospital, but he kept his eyes closed. Quietly they pulled into the emergency entrance of the Johnson County Community Hospital.

Inside the emergency room, she started to follow Doug's stretcher down the long hallway. A nurse intercepted her. "I'm sorry. You can't go in there," she said. "You'll have to stay in the waiting area."

Tracy stared down the blinding white corridor as Doug disappeared through a door marked "X-ray." "Do you have a telephone I could use?" she asked. "I don't have any money."

The nurse nodded and led her to the desk. "Over here."

Tracy nodded and began to dial. When Granny answered, Tracy explained what had happened. Her mother was already at Granny's for supper. They said they'd leave for the hospital immediately.

Tracy collapsed in a turquoise plastic chair along the wall. Out-of-date magazines were scattered across a scratched coffee table in front of her. But she couldn't concentrate enough to read while she knew Doug was still in pain.

Suddenly Tracy jerked up straight. With Doug's leg in a cast, he would have to stay off his feet. But the trial would start in less than two weeks, no matter what.

For the first time in her entire twelve years, Tracy faced a frightening situation alone. Doug had always been there, taking the lead while she followed. But now she couldn't hide in Doug's shadow.

Tracy shivered in spite of the stuffy waiting room. She had never felt so alone. It was up to her to catch the real criminal now, all by herself. And soon.

4

Break-Ins

❧

Sunday morning Doug relaxed on Granny's sofa, surrounded by people like a king with his subjects. His mother hovered on one side, patting his arm from time to time. Tracy barely left his other side. She felt at fault for Doug's accident. If only she hadn't whispered so loud! Then Mr. Simms wouldn't have discovered them and startled Doug into falling.

Granny kept rearranging her favorite afghans and lap robes over Doug's legs. When she wasn't watching, he kicked them off, but she just piled them on thicker. Doug seemed relieved when the doorbell rang.

Andrew stood holding Granny's philodendron and Swedish ivy. "Here're your plants, Ella Mae. The ivy was really rootbound. That's why your drainage was so poor," Andrew said. "I put some rocks in the bottom and the pots should drain better now." He poked his head around the doorway. "How's the leg, Doug?"

"A lot better, Andy," Doug said. "Come in and join us."

Andrew shook his head. "I have some yard work to do. But I'll come back later to visit you, if it's all right with your grandmother." He looked questioningly at Granny.

Tracy blinked; she couldn't believe her eyes. Granny was *blushing*. "I'm sure Doug would be happy to have visitors."

"Yes. Well, then . . ." Andrew mumbled. "I'll see you later."

Doug chuckled as Granny closed the door. "What is poor Andy going to do after he's repotted all your plants, Granny?" he asked in mock concern. "He'll have to think up another excuse to visit you."

"Hogwash, Douglas Nelson!" She bustled out of the room.

Tracy's mother pointed a warning finger at him. "Don't tease Granny. I think her friendship with Andrew is nice." She lowered her voice. "If you make her self-conscious about it, she might not want him around at all. And that would be a loss for both of them."

Secretly Tracy wasn't so sure. Why did Granny need Andrew's friendship anyway? She had plenty of lady friends in the other apartments. Every week they had tea together and played bridge. Tracy thought that that should be enough for Granny.

And besides, Andrew was totally different from her grandfather. She wondered why Granny hadn't noticed.

Granny came back to the living room, carrying glasses of apple juice. "Here's a little something to help keep up your strength."

Tracy's mother glanced out the window. "It's such a pretty day for a walk. I love spring," she said.

Doug thumped his cast in disgust. "If it weren't for this dumb leg, Tracy and I could hike out to the farm this afternoon. We haven't been there for weeks."

"Somebody has," Granny said mysteriously.

"What are you talking about?" Tracy's hand jerked and she dribbled juice down her chin.

"Since the last renters moved out, I've checked on the farm from time to time. Lately I've noticed that some items are missing."

Tracy's mother sighed. "I wish we could all live out there. Then we could keep an eye on things." She gazed from Doug to Tracy. "Someday we're going to fix up the farm like it was when I grew up there. We'll farm the place ourselves and have a huge garden.''

Tracy smiled, but remained silent. Returning to the farm was her mother's big dream. However, the old house first needed major repairs to its heating and water systems. Tracy knew her mother had no idea where the money would come from for fixing it.

Suddenly Tracy remembered what Granny had said. ''What's turned up missing out at the farm?'' she asked.

Granny spread another afghan over Doug's shoulders. ''Just odd things. A ladder and some small tools are missing from the shed. The house was broken into, but as far as I can tell, only some dishes were taken. I called Sheriff Braden, but he didn't find anything.'' Her tone implied that she wasn't at all surprised.

The chime clock interrupted them, chiming twelve times. Granny drained her juice glass. ''Time to make us a little lunch, I guess.'' She headed for the kitchen, with Tracy's mother following her.

Doug whistled softly. ''I sure wish I could go out to the farm this afternoon.''

''It *is* a nice day for a walk,'' Tracy agreed, glancing out the window.

''I don't mean that. I wish we could investigate where the house and shed were broken into.'' Doug leaned forward eagerly. ''If we caught this burglar, it might turn out to be the same person who took the jewelry from Simms!''

Tracy hated to dampen his enthusiasm. ''Too bad you can't walk on that leg for a few days.'' The farm was a mile out of town, and neither her mother nor Granny owned a car. ''We'll have to forget about investigating the farmhouse.''

Doug's eyes glinted. ''*I* couldn't,'' he said, ''but *you* could.''

''Oh, no, I couldn't!'' Tracy shook her head firmly. ''And I won't. Not on your life. No way. The subject is closed.''

''But listen.'' Doug grabbed her arm. ''What if the burglar at the farm *is* the jewelry thief? Mom's trial is less than two weeks away. I can't make it out to the farm, so you'll have to.''

Tracy's stomach churned. ''Mom would see me if I tried to leave, and she wouldn't let me go out there alone. She'll be here all day today.''

''Who said anything about today?'' Doug asked. ''I was thinking about after school tomorrow.''

Tracy turned her back on him, hoping her panic didn't show.

''I hate being stuck here,'' Doug said, ''but someone has to look into it. You heard Mr. Sandler say that even the police have stopped hunting for anyone else.''

Tracy grasped at one final straw. "What makes you think that the break-ins at the farm have anything at all to do with the jewelry theft?"

"Just listen. If Mr. Simms and Jake are the thieves, they might use the farmhouse as a meeting place. Maybe they're pinning the blame on Mom to keep her away from the farm. Who knows? Maybe they plan to remove the antiques from the house."

The thought of tangling with a burglar at the farm made Tracy's temples throb. However, even though the odds were against it, Doug could be right. If anyone was going to check it out, she knew it was up to her.

"Okay." The word stuck in her throat. "I'll do it."

That night Tracy lay flat on her back in bed, cold and stiff as an icicle. When she finally slept, she dreamed of jails and burglars and falls from fire escapes. She woke more weary than when she had crawled into bed.

Monday morning passed with Tracy in a daze, still dreading the thought of going out to the farm alone. After eating only a few bites of lunch, she threw the rest away. While waiting for the dismissal bell, she paused to read the announcements on the bulletin board in the cafeteria.

Notices of play rehearsals and baseball practices filled the center of the board. Lost and found items were listed, as well as several things for sale. As she read, one paper caught her attention. It was an old sign-up sheet. It announced a freshman trip to River City to see a play. Students were instructed to meet on the front steps right after school to board the school bus together.

Halfway down the list, Tracy spotted Lisa Curran's scribbled signature. Tracy glanced at the date of the play and gasped. It had been last Monday evening—*the night of the robbery.*

Lisa was supposed to have left town Monday right after school on a class trip! Why had she, instead, hung around the jewelry store that afternoon? Tracy suspected she knew. Excitedly, she snatched the old notice and stuck it in her notebook to show Doug later.

After school she stood on the front steps, alone, her legs trembling. If she turned left, in fifteen minutes she'd be at Granny's. Turning right, she could walk a mile out of town to her grandparents' farm. With a sudden giant hiccup, Tracy turned right. She took ten dragging steps, each step slower than the one before.

Suddenly she stopped. "I can't do it! I can't!" Pivoting on her heel, she stalked down the street in the opposite direction.

When she came to the downtown business section, Tracy paused across the street from Simms

Jewelry Store. Mr. Simms stood in the doorway, rocking back and forth on his heels. Tracy squinted as she watched him. Sighing, she decided he looked more like a mean bullfrog than a thief. He didn't seem clever enough to plan a robbery.

But was she willing to take that chance and maybe let him get away with it? Was she going to pass up possibly valuable clues just because she was scared?

Tracy glanced at her watch—nearly four o'clock. She knew if she hurried, she could jog out to the farm, search quickly, and be back to Granny's by five-thirty. But only if she started right away.

She straightened her narrow shoulders, took a deep breath, and trotted back along Main Street to the edge of town. She followed the gravel road to the abandoned farm. By the time she reached it, she was breathing heavily and her damp knit shirt clung to her back.

Walking up the shady driveway, Tracy realized she had run off much of her tension. She surveyed the farmyard. At a glance, everything looked peaceful and undisturbed. The two-story white farmhouse stood like a guard over the barn and several outbuildings. The dark windows in the house reflected fleecy clouds as Tracy trudged up to the back door.

She rattled the doorknob, hoping the locked door meant there had been no more burglaries. Peering through the dusty window pane, she spotted some clay flowerpots and broken chairs on the porch.

A stronger breeze ruffled Tracy's damp hair. She slowly shook her head. It was hard to understand now why she had been so afraid of visiting the farm alone.

Strolling down the slope toward the barn, Tracy passed the tool shed. She sucked in her breath sharply. Instead of being snapped shut, the padlock on the shed hung open on its heavy chain. Only the heavy wooden bar was in place across the door. She forced her feet, one step at a time, toward the shed.

Lifting the wooden bar, she opened the creaky door and peered into the dark shed. Inching forward, she swung her arms in front of her, reaching for the dangling string connected to the light bulb. The door began to swing shut behind her, cutting off the May sunshine. Tracy jumped back and pushed the door open again.

She reached inside the shed for an empty paint can to prop open the door. Then she groped again inside for the light. Grasping the slender string, she gave it a yank. Nothing happened.

The bulb must have burned out, Tracy thought. Sunlight from the door only reached a few feet into the shed. Murky shadows wavered under the worktable that ran the length of the room.

Tracy's heart pounded painfully under her ribs. As her eyes grew accustomed to the dimness, she studied the cobwebby shed. Her eyes were drawn to one corner under a tiny, boarded-up window.

She inched closer. On the workbench below the window, she found a one-burner hot plate and tin coffee pot. Two fairly clean cups, a plate, and a small jar of instant coffee were next to it. Tracy wondered if these were the missing dishes Granny had mentioned.

A gust of wind rattled the door against the paint can. Tiny hairs prickled on the back of Tracy's neck, and she glanced nervously over her shoulder. Awkwardly, she moved along the workbench, but she found no more evidence of intruders. Standing up, she brushed the dirt from her knees and the cobwebs from her hair.

Without warning a stronger gust of wind knocked over the empty paint can. It rolled aside and the door banged shut. The shed was plunged into darkness. Tracy jumped as the heavy wooden bar dropped into place on the outside. Stumbling toward the door, she fought the panic that washed over her.

Forgetting her determination to remain calm, she beat on the shed door with both fists.

"Help me! Somebody, help me!" Her screams echoed in her ears.

Tracy kicked the door and pain shot up her leg.

She continued screaming, although she knew no one was close enough to hear her. Clawing wildly at the wooden door, splinters scraped her hands and pierced the flesh under her fingernails.

I can stand anything, she screamed inwardly, *except being trapped in a dark place again.*

Her terror brought it all back sharply—that day eight years ago she thought she had forgotten. Tracy had only been four years old. One evening while playing outdoors, she'd followed a striped kitten around the farmyard. It had stayed just beyond her grasping hands. Then the kitten scampered down a path behind the barn.

Tracy had followed close behind, through tall weeds that grew up around rusty machinery. She'd searched and called, trying to coax the kitten from its hiding place. Just as she decided to turn back, the ground beneath her feet suddenly disappeared.

She landed on a bed of dried leaves in the bottom of an abandoned well. She wasn't hurt, and at first hadn't been afraid at all. But when she tried to climb out, Tracy discovered the sides of the well were slimy. She couldn't climb more than a foot or two without slipping back to the bottom. She tried again and again. Then she began to scream . . . .

She screamed her grandfather's name over and over. Dusk turned into night. Tracy huddled, shaking, in the bottom of the well. The blackness of the hole terrified her, but she was too tired to scream anymore. She curled up on the leaves and fell asleep, exhausted.

A flashlight shining in her eyes and someone calling her name had awakened her. Her grandfather had slowly lowered a ladder into the well, climbed down, and carried her out. That evening, he had rocked her in front of the fireplace for hours.

Now, just recalling her grandfather's strong arms around her all those years ago calmed Tracy's hammering heart. She collapsed against the locked shed door. Trembling, she tried to think of an escape.

She crept across the dark shed to the boarded-up window. It was too small for her to wiggle through, even if she could pry off the boards. Breaking down the door was out of the question. The wooden bar across the outside was several inches thick.

Gradually she became aware of a feeble sliver of light slicing through the darkness. She felt her way to the gap where weak sunlight came between two loose boards.

She grabbed the bottom of one loose board and yanked. It snapped in half, throwing Tracy backwards onto the floor. She scrambled up. After breaking off the board next to it, she flopped on her stomach in front of the hole she'd made, and squirming against the dirt, she pushed herself through the hole.

Outside, Tracy stumbled to the front of the

shed. Brushing off her filthy shirt, she glanced toward the barn. As long as she was at the farm, she knew she ought to check it out too. After quickly glancing inside, she walked around in back. Oak leaves rustled overhead as she stared at the undisturbed weeds that still grew up around rusty old machinery.

Tracy was pretty sure she remembered where the abandoned well was, even after all those years. She could probably find it. She started forward through the grass, but abruptly changed her mind.

Turning back toward the road, she decided she'd been trapped in enough small dark places for one day.

5

A Hair-Raising Experience

After jogging from the farm to Granny's apartment, Tracy arrived with cramps in both legs. Inside, she collapsed into Granny's rocking chair while Doug gave her the third degree.

Tracy held up a weary hand. "It seems the shed's been used for meetings," she said, explaining about the cups and hot plate. "I didn't see anything that points to who it is, though."

"Then what took you so long out there?" Doug demanded. "I had to tell Granny and Mom what you were doing when you didn't show up for supper."

"You had us pretty worried," her mother added.

Tracy rocked slowly. "I got trapped in the

shed. The wind blew the door shut and the bar fell in place.'' She turned to her grandmother. ''I pried off two boards in the back of the shed to get out, but I'll go back and fix the hole.''

''Don't worry about that,'' Granny said, shaking her head. ''I'm just glad you got out all right.''

Tracy pleated her shirttail. ''At first I kind of panicked. I kept remembering when I was trapped in the dry well behind the barn.''

''I remember that!'' Doug cried. ''We were only four or five.''

''I'd forgotten about the old well,'' Granny said. ''Your grandfather covered it right after your accident.''

Tracy rubbed her bruised hands. ''I'll go back to the farm tomorrow after school and nail the boards back on. Since I was already late, I didn't take the time tonight.''

Tracy's mother sat needlepointing a new seat for a chair she'd refinished. ''I think I'd like to go with you tomorrow,'' she said. ''I haven't been out to the farm in ages.''

''Could you really?''

''I'll meet you outside the school tomorrow afternoon,'' her mother said. ''We can walk to the farm from there.''

The next day passed quickly for Tracy. Her homeroom time was spent discussing the annual school bazaar the next Friday night. Tracy wished she could still be a part of the bazaar. She and Doug had planned to run a hot dog booth together, like last year. But now with his broken leg, he couldn't help.

After school when Tracy emerged from the building, she searched the milling crowd for her mother. Puzzled, she finally spotted her waiting in the shadow of the school.

She noticed two older boys who pointed to her mother, then turned and stared at her. Tracy heard one sneering boy mutter "thief's kid." The other boy snickered.

Tracy bit off the angry words that rose in her throat. She fixed her face into a smile and joined her mother. Talking loudly as they left, Tracy hoped her mom hadn't noticed the boys.

When they reached the farmhouse, Tracy's mother pulled two keys from her jeans pocket. The old skeleton key fit the rusty lock in the door. The small shiny key was for the new deadbolt lock.

Together they stepped into the dim interior of the house. Neither the sunshine nor warmth penetrated the darkness there. Over the years enclosed porches had been added on three sides of the house. Even on the sunniest days the inner rooms were full of shadows.

Tracy's mother switched on the overhead light

in the kitchen. Instantly the shadows receded. As Tracy gazed around the old kitchen, she remembered the many evenings she and her grandfather had spent at the scarred oak table. She drank milk from her grandfather's mustache cup while they both devoured large soft raisin cookies. Looking back, those evenings assumed a magical feeling.

Tracy's mother broke into her thoughts. "Come into the living room. I want to show you what I'd been working on before . . . well, before everything happened." Her voice sounded eager, happier than in weeks, Tracy thought.

She followed her into the darkest of all the rooms. Switching on a circular fluorescent ceiling light, her mother stood back proudly. "I've been reweaving these two old cane chairs I found in a back room. The seats and backs had rotted clear through."

Tracy squatted by the chair. "It really looks professional, Mom. Just like new."

"For such a big house, we'll need lots of furniture," her mother replied. "Of course, we'll be moving out here soon."

Tracy continued to stare at the chair, but the pattern of the caning blurred. Her mother's dream for the future was to move back to the farm. She planned for it and talked about it constantly, but she wasn't very practical, Tracy felt.

"How can we think of moving out here, Mom?" Tracy asked. "This drafty old house must cost a fortune to heat in the wintertime. We don't need this much space for just the three of us. The water tastes funny too—probably the well and pipes need to be worked on."

As Tracy glanced up, she was almost sorry she'd spoken. The dreamy smile on her mother's face slowly faded. Her mouth drew into a thin stubborn line.

"I know things need fixing up," she said. "But we'll get all those things done somehow. Then we'll move out here. Maybe Granny would like to live with us too. She gets as lonely as I do sometimes."

Tracy wished it could happen, but she hated to see her mother count on an impossible dream. She was only going to end up disappointed. "Maybe you shouldn't plan on moving here. We hardly have enough money as it is. It just isn't a practical idea."

"So don't even try?" her mother argued. "Tracy, you're too young to be so practical, as you call it. Besides, sometimes your dreams are all that keep you going."

"But isn't it better not to pin your hopes on impossible dreams? It makes the disappointment so much worse."

Her mother didn't answer for so long that Tracy wondered if she'd heard her. Finally she turned, her eyes gleaming. "Who determines what dreams are impossible? Many of our inventions, like the telephone or airplane, were called impossible dreams once." Her mother sounded defiant. "You need dreams—something to believe in for a better future. If you believe hard enough, they *will* come true."

Tracy shrugged, feeling sorry for her mother. In her opinion, only hard work and a lot of money would make her mother's dream come true. At the moment, her mother didn't even have a job.

Tracy sat cross-legged on the dusty floor, wishing she had a job herself. "If only I had a way to make money like Doug does. The money from his magic shows helps quite a bit. I wish I got paid for working at Kids Korner." Slumped over, she remembered that she couldn't even volunteer there anymore. She rested her chin in the palm of her hand. "Maybe I should look for a different part-time job for the summer. One that pays, like maybe a paper route."

"Absolutely not." Her mother knelt in front of her. "Someday you hope to run a preschool. This is good experience for you. It could help make *your* dream come true someday." She squeezed Tracy's shoulders. "And that's more important than money."

Tracy had never considered her volunteering in

that way. "If only Doug hadn't broken his leg. We could have made some money at our hot dog booth Friday night," she said.

"Why not run the bazaar booth by yourself?" her mother asked.

"Oh, I couldn't do that."

"Why not? Maybe you've lived in Doug's shadow long enough." She ruffled Tracy's hair. "I know you love doing things together, but it'd be good for you to do something on your own for a change. Cast your *own* shadow."

Tracy considered her mother's words. "I don't know. . . ." Her tone was doubtful. "Maybe if I can think of something easier to sell. Running the hot dog booth really takes at least two people."

"Let's go back and talk to Granny about it. She often comes up with unusual ideas." Her mother stood up and dusted off her jeans.

Tracy pulled herself to her feet. "If *Andrew* isn't there, I can talk to Granny, you mean. Lately he's always there, taking up her time."

Tracy's mother cocked her head to one side. "I've never heard you talk that way. What's bothering you?"

"Nothing! I just think Granny already has enough friends. She doesn't need Andrew. And he acts so friendly to Doug, almost like he's his own grandson." Tracy's voice fell to a whisper. "As if anyone could replace Grandpa."

"You think Andrew is trying to take your grandfather's place with Granny?"

"Looks like it to me. It seems to me that *you* would care that he might marry Granny. Doesn't it matter that he might replace your own father?"

"Andrew and Granny are just good friends. If he did want to marry Granny, though, I would be pleased for her. She's been very lonely these last couple of years." She frowned slightly. "Are you sure that's why you're upset?"

"What do you mean?"

"Are you really thinking about Granny and Andrew? Or are you afraid that someday *I* will remarry and your father will be replaced, as you call it?"

Tracy gasped. Her mother remarry someday? She'd never thought of that possibility! She studied the slim, pretty woman standing in front of her. Her eyes narrowed. Could her mom be right? Was that what she was really upset about?

"I don't know . . ." Tracy mumbled, suddenly remembering her mother's dates with Mr. Cunningham. "Would you do that?"

"If I ever consider remarrying, believe me, you and Doug would be the first to know." Squeezing

Tracy's hand, she pulled her toward the door. "Right now, though, we'd better hammer some boards over that hole in the shed."

Fifteen minutes later, after pounding nine nails and both of her thumbs, Tracy had the hole boarded up. By unspoken agreement, she and her mother put serious talking aside. Laughing, they made up goofy limericks as they walked back to town. As they strolled through the business district, Tracy glanced at Simms Jewelry Store.

"Look!" she cried. "See that man coming out of the store?"

"The one in the gray suit?"

"Yes!" Tracy watched him saunter down the street and disappear around the corner. "That's the same man I noticed in Simms when Doug and I were there Saturday. He acted awfully suspicious. Have you seen him in the store before?"

Tracy's mother frowned. "I couldn't say. With those dark glasses, I didn't get a very good look at his face."

"We talked to Bert Benson that day, too. He was friendly, but Mr. Simms came out and yelled at him." Tracy snapped her fingers. "Maybe Bert would know the name of the man in the gray suit."

"Well, you're not going to ask him now," her mother declared. "The store's closed, and I don't want you bothering Bert." Tracy's mother walked briskly ahead. Catching up with her mother, Tracy still couldn't help wondering about the mysterious man in gray.

After supper that evening, Tracy reminded Doug about the bazaar Friday night. Doug mentioned that his friend, Aaron, had called and offered to share his booth selling caramel apples. All he'd have to do was sit and make change. Their mother protested that she didn't want Doug up on his broken leg that soon.

"I'll change her mind by Friday," Doug whispered to Tracy.

"No doubt." Tracy drummed her fingers on the table. "I just wish I could think of a good idea for a booth to run by myself."

Granny sipped her coffee thoughtfully. "What about this?" she asked, pointing to the foliage in her window. "I have some plants I could donate and I bet they'd sell. Those insect-eating plants."

"Are you sure?" Tracy was fascinated by Granny's Venus's-flytraps and cobra plants. "I love touching the flytraps and making them snap shut. Other kids would think an insect-eater was neat, too."

"You'd be doing me a favor to take them. I have more plants than I know what to do with," Granny said. "Just repot them into styrofoam cups so I can keep the clay pots."

"Right away!" Tracy said, moving to the window. She touched the trigger hair on the edge of a hinged flytrap. It snapped shut. She knew it would open again in twenty-four hours, though, since there was no food in the trap.

"Before you start," Doug interrupted, "do you want to see some new tricks I've been practicing for my next party?"

Actually she didn't, but Tracy felt sorry for Doug being stuck in the apartment all day. "Sure," she said, trying to sound enthusiastic.

Just then Andrew rang the doorbell. "Just in time to see Doug's newest science tricks," Granny said, inviting him in.

Doug cleared his throat and bowed dramatically from his chair. "These tricks deal with static electricity. The first trick is called 'snake charmer.' I put different lengths of thread on this table here. These are the snakes. Then I'll charge this comb by rubbing it on this piece of wool."

After doing so, he held the charged comb over the threads and moved it back and forth. The colored threads rose up on end, dancing on the table as the comb waved about them.

After applauding wildly, Tracy started to leave, but Doug motioned her back down. "Just one more."

"I don't know what could possibly top snake charming," Tracy said.

"This will," Doug assured her. "You can be my assistant."

Tracy bowed to their audience and sat by Doug's chair. After rubbing a balloon against the carpet, Doug held it over Tracy's head. Wispy strands of her hair stood up.

Granny laughed. "You look like you've seen a ghost, Tracy."

Doug drawled, "I call this a *hair-raising* experience."

Tracy rolled her eyes toward the ceiling and batted the balloon away. "Seriously, those aren't bad tricks. I guess little kids like tricks that they can copy at home."

"When's your next party?" Andrew asked. "I'd love to see you perform."

Doug leaned back in his chair, the smile fading from his face. "I don't know. I haven't been able to book a kid's party since Bryan Simms's seventh birthday." He glanced guiltily at his mother. "Sorry, I didn't mean to bring up their names."

"Don't worry about it," his mother said, staring out the window. Thick silence filled the room.

"When was his birthday?" Andrew asked, breaking the awkward stillness. "Recently?"

"No, he was seven on Valentine's Day," Doug said. "He had all these dumb heart decorations. I'd hate to have my birthday on Valentine's Day. That junk's for girls."

Smiling, Tracy picked up three Venus's-flytrap plants and three cobra plants to repot outside. Watching Doug, she shook her head regretfully. He wasn't a bad magician. Too bad he couldn't use his magic act to conjure up the missing jewelry.

6

The Man in Gray

On Wednesday evenings in the warmer months, Centerville's stores and library stayed open until nine o'clock. Walking uptown on a Wednesday night always marked the real beginning of spring weather and Tracy was anxious to go.

Doug protested from the sofa. "I'm stuck here all day! The least you could do is stay and play Cribbage with me."

Tracy tucked in her shirt. "But I need to go uptown. I'm making a poster about insect-eating plants for my display at the bazaar."

"You have some poster board already," Doug said, pointing an accusing finger at his twin. "I saw you bring it home from school."

"I know, but I'm going to the library to look up things—like what causes the jaws of the flytrap to shut and hold together, and what digestive enzymes are produced in the cobra plants," Tracy explained. "And kids will want to know how big the plants will get, and what to feed them when there's a shortage of insects and—"

"Okay, okay." Doug heaved a long sigh. "If you must . . . ."

Tracy slipped on her jacket and laughed. "I must," she assured him.

Her mother finished rinsing dishes at the sink. "Mind if I walk along with you? I need to stop at Willard's for more embroidery floss," she said. "Anyway, I don't want you walking home alone after dark."

Tracy waited outside on the step, glad her mom was coming with her. They used to do so many things together, just the two of them. Since the arrest, though, there hadn't been much time.

Soon Tracy and her mother were strolling down the cracked and humpy sidewalk. The street was filled with shoppers. Ladies chatted on corners while babies dozed in strollers. Men swapped stories in front of the hardware store.

They stopped in front of the library. "I'll meet you back here at eight o'clock after I do my shopping," her mother said. "That gives you an hour and a half to do your research. Think that's enough time?"

"Sure. I can always check out the books if I don't get done."

"Fine. If you finish early, just wait for me inside."

Tracy nodded and watched her mother start down the street. She admired her courage. She knew her mom must dread going into stores after all the bad publicity. People were bound to stare at her.

Tracy bounced up the library's cracked steps, patting the stone lions that guarded the entrance. It would be nice—at least for a while—to think of something as impersonal as insect-eating plants.

After searching the card catalog, Tracy went to the main room for her science books. The spacious room also doubled as a reading room. Magazine racks and daily newspapers were grouped at one side of the room. Andrew sat reading a paper at one large table. Tracy had mixed feelings about seeing him there. She saw enough of him at Granny's apartment, but she figured it wouldn't hurt to say hello.

She tiptoed up beside him. "Hi, Andrew," she whispered, glancing at the others reading. "Nice night to walk uptown, isn't it?"

Andrew smiled and leaned over his newspaper. "Always feels good to get some exercise," he agreed pleasantly.

Tracy glanced at the open newspaper and noted

that Andrew was reading the society page. "Anything interesting?" she asked.

He spread his bony arms across the paper. "No, not much."

Tracy smiled inwardly. She'd always thought that only women were interested in the society page. Mostly it was filled with stories of church luncheons, bridal showers, and wedding announcements.

Suddenly Andrew sneezed, his arm jerking aside. Tracy glimpsed a picture at the top of the page. Mr. and Mrs. Leonard Simms were announcing their twentieth wedding anniversary. She leaned closer. The article said that their children were giving them an open house on Sunday.

Tracy straightened, sorry to be reminded of Mr. Simms. Grudgingly, she appreciated Andrew's attempt to keep her from seeing the picture.

"I'd better get busy. I'm looking up stuff about insect-eating plants," Tracy said. She moved away toward the stacks of books. By the time she located her three books, Andrew was gone. Tracy was surprised, but not exactly sorry.

Unwillingly, Tracy recalled her mother's words at the farm. Could her mother be right about why Andrew vaguely bothered her? Was she truly thinking about Granny? Or was she really afraid that her own mother might find someone to replace her father? As much as Tracy hated to think so, her mother's question had struck a nerve.

Shaking her head, she spread the biology books around her. Soon she was engrossed in her reading. She discovered that the Venus's-flytrap's jaws snapped shut in one twentieth of a second. Pitcher plants attracted insects with a sweet substance in their pitchers. Sundew plants, on the other hand, caught insects by wrapping their tentacles around them.

By seven o'clock Tracy had more than enough notes. Using tracing paper, she copied pictures of the various plants to use for illustrations on her posters. After reshelving the books, she glanced at the clock.

There were still forty-five minutes until her mother was due back. Reading a magazine didn't sound inviting. Tracy gazed longingly out the library windows as group after group of kids and adults strolled by.

She wondered idly if the mysterious man in gray was in town too. If only she could ask Bert Benson about him. Suddenly she snapped her fingers. Even though she should stay at the library, she knew she could go to Simms and be back easily by eight o'clock.

However, her stomach flip-flopped at the idea

of questioning Bert alone. He was a friend of her mother's, though, and would surely help if he could. Patting her sweater pocket, she made sure that her small notebook and pencil were there. If Bert said something worth remembering, she wanted to report his exact words to Doug when she got home.

In front of the library, she searched north and south. She couldn't spot her mother in front of any of the stores, so she set off briskly through the settling dusk.

Rounding the corner, Tracy slid to a halt. Andrew sat on a bench at the bus depot half a block away. All she needed was for Andrew to see her and tell Granny. She started to back up, but he was already waving to her. Reluctantly, she dragged herself over to the bench.

"Hello, again. Are you just sitting here or are you going someplace?" Tracy asked.

She read the large sign in front of the depot announcing bus departures and arrivals. The depot shared a building with the Clover Leaf Cafe. Beside the bus schedule, another sign announced split pea and ham as the soup of the day.

"I'm on my way to the River City library." Andrew pointed at the schedule which announced a 7:34 departure. "I want some books about the Old West and railroads that our library doesn't have."

"Looks like your ride is on time," Tracy said,

nodding at the light blue bus rounding the corner. Its air brakes whooshed as it stopped in front of the bench. "Have a nice ride, Andrew," she added, turning toward Centerville's business block.

A glance at the courthouse clock made her quicken her steps. She had barely half an hour to question Bert and return to the library.

When she was half a block from Simms Jewelry Store, Tracy spotted a shadowy figure slip out of the store. Light from a street lamp revealed it was Lisa Curran. She didn't look much like a girl with a shoplifting record.

Tracy hid in the shadow of the Orpheum Theater and watched Lisa. She sauntered down the sidewalk, pausing several times to stare at window displays before she evaporated into the crowd. Recalling the field trip notice, Tracy wondered again what had happened the night of the robbery.

Her mother still didn't believe Lisa had taken the jewelry, even after Tracy told her that Lisa had skipped a school trip that afternoon. Calling it circumstantial evidence, her mom still refused to tell the police about her.

Tracy moved quickly down the street to the alley next to Simms. She wondered where in the building Bert was working. It was out of the question to go into the store and ask for him. Her knees quivered just thinking about it.

Wandering partway down the alley, she noticed a door under the fire escape marked "Keep Out." Garbage cans and empty boxes were stacked next to the door. Her heart thumping wildly, Tracy inched over to the door and tapped softly.

When no one answered, she stiffened her shaking legs and knocked again. No sounds came from inside. Letting out her breath, she turned from the door. She was relieved to hurry back to the safety of the library.

Before she could, Tracy heard the door open behind her. She turned and saw Bert poking his head out the door. "Oh, it's you. Miss Nelson, right?"

"Uh, yes," Tracy said, reaching for her pencil and notebook. "Do you mind if I ask you a couple more questions, Mr. Benson?"

Bert looked up and down the alley. "I'll help if I can," he said. "But I didn't work the night the robbery took place. I never work nights."

Tracy shivered and hiccuped. "Well, actually I have a question about a man I've seen a couple times in the jewelry store. Both times he was dressed in gray, with a dark hat and sunglasses." She flipped through her notebook for exact dates. "I saw him last Saturday and again yesterday afternoon. Do you know who he is?"

Bert fingered a chain attached to his overalls.

"Think I know who you mean. Don't know his name. Once saw him get off the bus from River City."

"Why would he come to a Centerville store to shop? River City's stores are so much bigger." Remembering the man's empty hands, Tracy added, "I don't think he even bought anything."

In a low voice, Bert whispered, "Now that you mention it, that man's in the store right now. At least he was ten minutes ago." Bert pulled the chain on his overalls and a pocket watch appeared. He snapped it open. "Store closes in twenty minutes. He might still be there."

"Thanks a lot." She turned and crept back up the alley. The door closed behind her with a faint metallic click.

Pausing at the entrance to the darkened alley, Tracy searched the sidewalks. Her mother was still nowhere in sight, but Tracy knew her time was running out. In fact, her mother could be at the library already. And yet, she didn't dare leave. This man in gray might be the clue they'd been hoping for.

Tracy slid around the corner of the jewelry store, her back pressed to the brick building. Light from its front window cast faded orange rectangles on the sidewalk. Darkness had settled quickly over the small town.

Two women stared at her as they passed. Tracy pasted a half-smile on her lips and strolled to the window, stopping just short of the yellow patches of light. Hoping she appeared casual, Tracy held her breath and peeked around the corner of the window.

A quick glance showed a nearly empty store. The new clerk stood with her back to the window, showing an elderly lady a sparkling ring. Mr. Simms was working at his desk. With a combination of disappointment and relief, Tracy saw no sign of her mysterious man in gray.

Just as she turned to leave, he stepped out from behind a rotating display of watches. Tracy jerked back. Careful to keep in the shadows, she watched his movements. He strolled about the store, apparently looking at the jewelry counters. Once, while examining leather billfolds, he glanced briefly out the front window.

Tracy ducked. Crouching, she waited for the pounding in her ears and chest to stop. Slowly she rose until her eyes were level with the bottom of the window. She saw with alarm that "Mr. Gray" was striding toward the door!

Tracy darted around the corner of the building into the dark alley. She ran ten steps and dived behind an empty garbage can. Panting, she peered around the trash container.

The muscles in Tracy's neck began to cramp from holding her head at an odd angle. She hoped her mysterious stranger would come out of the store and turn in the other direction. The faint tinkle of the door chimes floated into the alley. Catching her breath, she heard soft footsteps on the sidewalk.

Tracy ducked down as "Mr. Gray" crossed the alley. He looked neither right nor left, evidently in a hurry to get someplace. The bus depot maybe? Tracy slipped out of her hiding place and hurried to the entrance of the alley.

Tracy watched Mr. Gray march briskly down the street. Shoppers filled the sidewalks as stores prepared to close. He zigzagged expertly through the maze of people. Tracy gratefully melted into the crowd, sure she could follow "Mr. Gray" without being spotted.

When he reached the corner, he turned right without a backward glance. Tracy wondered if he were going to catch the 8:05 bus. He was going in the depot's direction. She quickened her steps.

Just then Mrs. Billows, Tracy's math teacher, stepped out of the drug store. "Hello there, Tracy!" Mrs. Billows blocked her view of the corner. "What brings you uptown this lovely evening?"

Tracy groaned inwardly and inched around her teacher. "Nothing much," she said. "Just a little work at the library."

Mrs. Billows beamed as if Tracy had said something really clever. "How nice! How nice!"

Smiling and waving, Tracy turned and broke

into a run until she reached the end of the block. Peeking around the corner, she sucked in her breath sharply. He was gone!

Tracy pivoted to the right, then the left, confused. She *knew* he had turned that way. Even in the side street's murky shadows Tracy could see well enough. Only an old woman hobbled down the sidewalk a block away. No one else was in sight.

Tracy hesitated. Where had he disappeared? He must have had a car parked on this side street, she decided. For the hundredth time, Tracy wished Doug was with her. *He* wouldn't have lost "Mr. Gray." If only she had seen the man's car. At least she could have copied his license in her notebook. Then they would have had some real evidence to show to the police.

Sighing, she continued down the street. The library was two blocks ahead. She had ten minutes to get there and find a magazine to read. She hoped desperately that her mother wouldn't be early.

Deep in thought, Tracy fingered the rough brick on the side of the hardware store. No cars were parked along the side street. The alley running behind the Main Street stores was deserted and dark. Glancing over her shoulder, Tracy tried to whistle. Instead she began to hiccup.

Later, she thought that if she had been facing forward, she might have seen it. But she didn't even glimpse the gloved hand that reached out of the overgrown bushes. A strong arm yanked her roughly off the sidewalk and dragged her into an apartment house entry.

Tracy drew a deep breath to scream. The hand clamped over her open mouth, hard. The scream died in her throat.

7

Closing In

Tracy lashed out with both fists. Twisting from side to side, she struggled to breathe. The gloved hand tightened over her mouth and nose. She was afraid if she fought any longer, the stranger would suffocate her. Tracy suddenly went limp.

The hand relaxed its grip. "That's better," a hoarse voice whispered from behind her. "Don't scream. I won't hurt you."

Tracy nodded her head with difficulty. Slowly the man pulled his hand from her face. He waited, his hand close to her mouth. When Tracy remained quiet, the hand dropped.

Two hands gripped her arms from behind and spun her around. Tracy stared up into the face of "Mr. Gray."

Shaking, she tried to put a steel edge on her voice. "What do you want?" she demanded. The breathy words held a slight quiver.

The man pushed back his hat brim and the dim light from the doorway shone on his face. "I might ask the same question, don't you think? Haven't you been following me?"

Tracy's heart hammered in the night's stillness.

His next words shocked Tracy. "You just blew the only chance to clear your mother of the theft charges."

"What? Why? What are you talking about?"

The man's voice hardened. "I was the only one hunting for the real thief. No one else even believes your mother is innocent."

Tracy backed up a step. "Who *are* you?"

The man reached into a pocket inside his jacket. He pulled out a wallet and opened it. On one half was the man's picture; on the other half, words were typed.

Tracy peered closely and read: "Craig Daniel Whitaker, Private Investigator. River City, Michigan." Other information was in print too small to read. Tracy peered up at him. She had never seen a private eye's official papers before. She bet it wouldn't be hard to make false papers.

"Are you saying that you're a private investigator? You're working for Mr. Sandler to help clear my mother?" she asked suspiciously.

"I *was*," he corrected her. "Not anymore. You blew my cover. Asking questions about me was bad enough. But Mr. Simms spotted you outside the window tonight watching me. He asked to see my ID. There's no use in nosing around here anymore."

With a sickening sinking feeling, Tracy knew he was telling the truth. She had ruined everything in her clumsy attempt at playing detective.

Mr. Whitaker scratched his thinning hair. "You've got spunk, trying to find the thief on your own. But I wish Mr. Sandler had warned you about me." He poked his head out the door.

"Going back to River City?" Tracy asked.

"No point in sticking around town now." The man squinted at the lighted dial of his watch. "If I hurry, I can catch the 8:05."

"The 8:05?" Tracy gasped. "What time is it?"

"7:58. Why?"

"I'm supposed to meet my mom at eight o'clock," she said in a rush. "You know, I'm sorry about messing up your disguise. I'd give anything not to have ruined it all."

The man nodded and tipped his hat. Then he cut across the street at an angle and jogged toward the bus depot.

Tracy raced to the library, stumbling up the cement steps. Panting, she pushed open the doors. The librarian looked up from her desk. "The library is closing, Tracy." She glanced pointedly at the clock.

"I know," Tracy said, catching her breath. "I left something here. Has my mom been in yet?"

"No, I don't think so."

Tracy thanked her and hurried into the main room. Her books and notes were on the table where she'd left them. She grabbed the current issue of *Bird World,* flipped it open, and flopped into a chair. Five minutes later her mother rushed into the quiet library.

"Hi, honey. I'm sorry I'm late. I ran into Mrs. Phillips at the department store and we got to talking. She was so friendly—not like a lot of people—and we had a nice visit."

Tracy gathered up her books, grateful to Mrs. Phillips for delaying her mother. "That's okay. Really."

Walking home, they discussed the school's annual bazaar. Tracy discovered that her mother didn't intend to come. She said she didn't want to embarrass Doug and her. Tracy protested, although she knew they would get a lot of stares. Her mother finally agreed to consider coming.

The next afternoon at school was set aside for

transforming the gym into a festive bazaar. Hurrying to the gym, Tracy claimed a small card table for her display. Signs around the gym announced baked goods, ceramics, helium balloons, and other items for sale.

Tracy spotted Bert hanging purple and orange streamers from the ceiling. She remembered Granny saying that Bert did extra handyman chores at the school.

Granny and Andrew arrived with Tracy's insect-eating plants at two o'clock. By then she had arranged her posters and covered her table with a green cloth. Suddenly excited, she was glad she had a booth of her own after all.

Tracy looked up from arranging her plants. "Where's Mom, Granny? With her lawyer?"

Granny slid the empty box under the table. "I think your mother's out at the farmhouse. She spends a lot of time—" Granny suddenly waved as Bert walked by with his ladder. "Yoo-hoo! Bert! I have a favor to ask you."

"What is it?" he asked, ambling over to Tracy's table.

"Could you come by my apartment on Saturday? You remember where it is?" When the janitor nodded, Granny asked, "Could you put on my screens? Summer will be upon us soon."

Bert nodded. "Sure, Mrs. Taylor, but I can't come until the afternoon. I'm helping take down these decorations in the morning."

Granny beamed at him. "The afternoon is just fine. Plan to stay for tea and fresh apricot bread when you finish."

Bert smiled and moved to the exit. He held the double doors open as Doug hobbled into the gym on crutches. Following behind Doug was his best friend, Aaron Wilson. Tracy knew they had come to set up their caramel apples booth.

Granny waved goodbye and moved off with Andrew in Doug's direction. Tracy decided to wander around the gym to inspect the other booths.

She remembered last year's bazaar and how the gym had looked at night. Colored streamers blowing, the aroma of fresh popcorn, the jostling crowds. It reminded her of a miniature carnival, and suddenly she couldn't wait for Friday night.

At one booth, Tracy wished she could afford to buy the corn husk doll sitting in a swing. She would tell her mother it was for decorating the farmhouse when they moved in. Tracy still doubted the move would ever actually take place, but she was beginning to understand her mother's need to believe in a dream.

At a ceramics booth across the gym, Tracy

studied the painted cats and birds on display. Two girls worked behind the table, their backs to her. They unpacked carefully wrapped ceramic pieces.

"We'd be set up by now if Lisa had come," muttered the tall brunette with barrettes.

"Isn't that just like her?" the blonde whispered, unwrapping another bowl. "Just like when she didn't show up for the class trip on Monday."

Tracy snapped to attention. They must be talking about Lisa Curran! She didn't recall any other Lisas on the class trip list.

The brunette shook her head. "My mother would never have driven me to River City if *I'd* missed the bus!"

"Not that she saw much of the play anyway," the blonde interrupted. "She left when it was half over. I *heard* she was sick."

The brunette snorted loudly. "With what? Kleptomania?"

Tracy's hand froze over a tiger figurine. So Lisa made it to River City Monday after all. What excuse had she given her mother for missing the bus? Tracy doubted if Lisa'd told her mother she'd been trying on jewelry. Or *shoplifting* it.

A sudden thought made Tracy gasp.

Suppose Lisa *had* taken the jewelry after school that day. She could have taken it to River City with her. Then, when pretending to be sick during the play, she could have slipped out of the building.

Tracy knew River City had three pawn shops. Could the missing jewelry be in a River City pawn shop at that very minute?

Tracy pivoted on her heel. She had to talk to Doug right away!

8

The Bazaar

Tracy scanned the crowded room, but her brother was no longer in sight. The caramel apples booth appeared finished. Doug and Aaron must have gone home, she decided in disappointment.

That night at Granny's apartment, she cornered her brother and whispered what she had discovered. "It must be Lisa Curran they were talking about," she finished. "If she *is* a kleptomaniac, maybe we can catch her in the act. Let's watch her like a hawk at the bazaar Friday night."

Doug agreed. Even if they didn't catch Lisa red-handed, they decided it was time to convince their mother to report Lisa's actions.

At the gym Friday night, Tracy stumbled through the crowd that flowed through its doors.

The blinking lights overhead almost seemed to make her red shirt glitter. After about twenty minutes, Tracy was pleased to see her mother come in with Granny. Her mother was her first customer and she carried her Venus's-flytrap away proudly, showing it to several people she met.

Tracy tried several times to spot Lisa, but the crowd was too thick and kept shifting. For the first hour Tracy was kept busy explaining the care and feeding of insect-eating plants. Between customers she chased away little boys who kept touching the flytraps to make them snap shut. Once she caught a glimpse of Doug hobbling on crutches through the crowd. She also noticed Bert carrying in buckets of ice for the lemonade and punch stand.

Tracy was almost glad when the crowd thinned out in her area; she needed to go get additional change from the principal. She glanced up after straightening her booth.

Five feet away, Lisa Curran stood watching her.

As Tracy stared back, Lisa's glance dropped. She turned as if to leave, but hesitated. Then, holding her head high, she marched up to Tracy's booth.

Tracy hiccuped. "Do you want to buy a plant?" she asked.

Lisa twisted the tail of her bright red shirt into

a knot. "Maybe I shouldn't have come."

"Why?" Tracy asked. "Why shouldn't you be here?"

"I know what people say about me." Lisa looked her directly in the eye. "But your mother was different. She was my friend, so I want you to know something."

Tracy's pulse quickened. She didn't speak, afraid that the timid-looking older girl would vanish into the crowd.

Lisa leaned close to Tracy. In a tense whisper, she said, "I *know* your mother didn't steal the jewelry!"

"How do you know?"

"I saw something at the jewelry store. Something suspicious," she hissed. "I think I know who stole the jewelry."

"*Who?*" Tracy jerked back, knocking over one of her plants.

Before she could answer, two girls from Tracy's English class pushed to the front of her booth. Laughing and pointing, they demanded to be shown the Venus's-flytrap eating a bug. Lisa started to edge away, and Tracy was afraid there'd be no more time to talk privately.

She motioned Lisa over to the table. "Can you meet me at the public library tomorrow morning at nine o'clock? We could talk then."

"I . . . I guess so," Lisa mumbled. "I want to help your mother. I know she's innocent."

For the rest of the evening, Tracy smiled at customers as if she were a robot. All she could think about were Lisa's words. *I know your mother didn't steal the jewelry. I saw something.* For the first time since the theft, Tracy felt real hope.

When the last customer left, Tracy propped up a sign that read: "Back in five minutes." She *had* to talk to Doug. Finally—the break they'd been waiting for! By the next morning she could have enough evidence to clear their mother.

Tracy zigzagged through the crowd to the caramel apple booth. Hopping from one foot to the other, she finally caught Doug's eye. He hurried the customers through, then drew Tracy aside.

"Guess what?" he cried. "Have I got news for you! You remember that kid, Bryan Simms, Mr. Simms's son?" Doug didn't wait for Tracy to answer. "He said they're moving! Their house is up for sale. He said his dad has to sell the store." His eyes gleamed. "I guess we were right. It sounds like Mr. Simms is in worse money trouble than we thought. He probably stole the jewelry himself for the insurance money."

"That's great! I wonder if Mom's lawyer knows?" Tracy snapped her fingers. "I have some news too. I just talked to Lisa Curran—"

"Hey, Doug! Lend me a hand, will you?" Aaron Wilson called. "I need some more apples from the refrigerator."

"Coming!" Doug shifted his crutches. "I'll talk to you back at Granny's later. Are you walking home with Mom?"

Tracy nodded. "We'll leave around nine, I think. Granny and Mom are here somewhere. Get home quick—my news will make your day!"

"I'll probably beat you. I'm riding home with Aaron." With a thumbs-up signal, Doug hobbled away to the cafeteria's refrigerator.

Twenty minutes later, Granny and Tracy's mother strolled up to her booth. "How's business?" her mother asked.

Tracy leaned on her elbows. "It was busy earlier, but I think I'm about finished. I only have four little plants left."

Granny looked at the thinning crowd. "Are you about ready to go home? Doug and Aaron are already finished and cleaning up."

Tracy nodded. "I'm going to straighten up now too, but I've changed my mind about walking. I decided to catch a ride with Doug and Aaron. I want to talk to Doug about something."

"I guess that's okay," her mother said slowly. "We'll see you at the apartment. Come straight home."

In ten minutes Tracy had taken down her posters and boxed her remaining plants. Waving across the gym at her brother, she took her rolled-up posters and stored them in her locker.

Breathless, she trotted back to the gym, but Doug and Aaron were no longer in sight. Their booth was completely empty. Tracy raced to the parking lot, but the Wilsons' blue station wagon was gone. If only she'd told Doug earlier she wanted to ride with them.

She looked up at the clear, sparkling sky. At least it was a nice night for a walk, she thought. Strolling along Main Street, she glanced in several store windows. At Simms Jewelry Store, she was startled to see a shadow moving around in the back. She stepped quickly to the window and peered in, but it was only Bert. It looked as if he were shampooing the rug.

"Must be making the store look better to sell it," Tracy thought.

Without warning, a bony finger dug into her shoulder blade. Shrieking, Tracy jumped forward and hit the plate glass window.

Turning, she found the building's night watchman towering over her. "You scared me!" she cried.

"Sorry," he growled. He raised his arm, showing a coiled snake tattoo. "Why don't you go home? Or I'll report you for loitering."

"I wasn't loitering," Tracy said, hiccuping.

"Scram!" The watchman advanced toward her. "And stop snooping around here!"

Tracy jumped, then turned and raced toward home, her heart pounding furiously. She covered two blocks before slowing down with a painful stitch in her side. Hunched over, she shuddered as she remembered the night watchman's scowl.

The quiet night gradually calmed her thoughts and ragged breathing. In ten minutes she was at Granny's back door where she slipped gratefully inside.

Vaguely Tracy was aware of voices coming from the living room. She breathed deeply for a minute, knowing she was in trouble for walking home alone. Resigned to a lecture, she went to join her family.

In the living room, Granny, Doug, and Andrew sat motionless. Granny glanced up at Tracy. "Where have you been?" she asked, sounding more worried than angry.

"I missed a ride with Doug and Aaron and had to walk home. I'm sorry I upset you." Tracy rubbed her hand across her tired eyes.

Granny didn't seem to hear her answer. "You'd better sit down and hear the news." Her voice sounded flat, unbelieving.

"What news?"

"Your mother was at the farmhouse last night, working on some old furniture," Granny said. "She was alone. She can't prove she was there."

Tracy glanced at Doug, but he stared at the floor. "Why does she need to prove where she was last night?" Tracy stammered.

Doug sighed and looked up. "There was another robbery at Simms last night." He paused, smashing his fist against his cast. "Mom's being questioned about it. The police picked her up a few minutes ago."

9

Time Runs Out

"Another robbery?" Tracy collapsed into a chair.

Doug nodded miserably. "If only one of us had been with Mom out at the farm last night. Then we could prove where she was."

Tracy glanced around the room. Granny twisted a handkerchief into knots. Andrew sat with his hands hanging limply beside him. Doug clenched and unclenched his hands.

Tracy slapped herself on her forehead. "Wait a minute!" she cried. "I almost forgot to tell you."

"Tell us what?" Doug asked sharply.

"Tonight, at the bazaar, Lisa Curran came to my booth to tell me she was sure Mom hadn't stolen the jewelry. She'd seen something suspicious at the store and wanted to tell me." She beamed at the eager faces around her.

Andrew broke the spell. "What exactly did she tell you?"

"Well, nothing yet." When Tracy saw the disappointment on Granny's face, she hurried on. "She's going to meet me tomorrow morning so we can talk more privately."

Heavy silence filled the tiny apartment. The only sounds Tracy heard were the ticking of the wall clock and Andrew's wheezy breathing. Granny and Doug exchanged an oddly frightening glance.

"What's the matter?" she demanded. "Don't you think it's good news? Mom said Lisa spent a lot of time at the jewelry store. She could've seen something important that will help Mom."

"She might have," Doug agreed, his mouth in a grim line, "but she may never tell you what it was."

"Why not?"

Doug took a deep breath. "Because tonight Lisa was hit by a car. She's unconscious. She was taken to River City Hospital."

Tracy gasped. "How did it happen?"

"Aaron and I were riding home down Cherry Street with his dad. When we saw the rescue squad lights flashing up ahead, we stopped to help. The rescue team said Lisa was a hit-and-run victim."

"I can't believe it! I just talked to her an hour ago!" Tracy studied Doug's troubled face. "You don't believe it was an accident, do you, Doug? Do you think she was hit on purpose—to keep her from telling what she knew?"

"I don't know," Doug answered. "But it certainly will keep her quiet, won't it?"

Tracy shivered. "Do you think someone overheard us making plans to meet tomorrow?" she asked slowly. "Maybe the hit-and-run driver was someone at the bazaar!"

Doug shrugged hopelessly. "That narrows it down to about three hundred people or so."

"Maybe we could go to River City in the morning," Tracy suggested. "Lisa's doctor might let us see her if we say it's an emergency. With Mom's trial starting next week, it *is* an emergency."

"You must be fourteen to visit a patient," Granny interrupted. "I could go, but I'm sure they wouldn't let me question her. Even if she pulls through, she'll be terribly weak for a long time."

"I know you're right. It's just that I'd thought I was so close to clearing Mom. And now this." Selfish or not, her shock over the accident was mingled with a terrible disappointment.

Andrew pulled himself wearily to his feet. "I'd better go, Ella Mae." He waved half-heartedly to Tracy and Doug, then left quietly. Granny walked with him to the kitchen door.

Tracy moved close to Doug, an awful idea crossing her mind. "I just thought of something. Lisa and I were both wearing red shirts tonight. Do you think the hit-and-run driver meant to hit *me*?"

Doug shoved his hair back off his forehead. "I don't know, Tracy. I hate to think so, but you could be right—if someone overheard you talking to Lisa tonight. If only I didn't have this stupid cast on my leg! I can't track down any clues this way."

Tracy chewed her thumbnail. "Maybe we have enough clues and information already, and just don't know it," she said. "I've taken careful notes of everything that's happened and the people we talked to."

"Maybe you're right. Let's read through your notes right now," Doug said.

Tracy reached into her right pocket, then dug deep into her left pocket. Her forehead creased into a frown. "I guess I forgot to put the notebook in my pocket. Maybe I just left it in Granny's room." Tracy ran out of the room and returned in less than a minute. "It isn't there either. I'm sure I didn't lose it. Do you think someone took it?"

"It wouldn't surprise me. I'm sure Mr. Simms is mixed up somehow in the thefts. He didn't like you taking notes the day we talked to him." Doug cracked three of his knuckles. "Think back. When do you remember last seeing the notebook?"

Tracy thought back over the last few days. She

distinctly remembered having it Tuesday at the farmhouse when she repaired the hole in the shed. "I guess the notebook could have dropped out without my noticing it."

"Good thing it's in code. Most people don't know Braille. Tomorrow you'll go out to the farm and find it."

"Oh, no, I won't! I'm not going out there alone again. I'm finished playing detective without any help."

"But you have to. I'd go if I could. You know I would." He gripped her arm. "Your notebook may hold the key to the real thief. We can't let Mom down."

"I know, but—but—" Finally Tracy nodded slowly. If only they could go to the police with their suspicions. But so far, all they had were guesses.

Saturday morning was overcast and gloomy. Tracy started to explain her plans to Granny about returning to the farm, but was interrupted by Andrew's knock at the back door. He announced that he was ready to help Granny transplant her seedlings.

"Thank you, Andrew." Granny pulled on her gardening gloves. "Tracy is going to help us, too, aren't you, Tracy?" Tracy glanced up in surprise.

"It will help to keep our hands busy. It won't help your mother for us to sit all day and worry."

Tracy nodded, embarrassed at the rush of relief she felt. She was glad to put off going to the farm until the afternoon.

For two hours they transplanted tomatoes in the garden in front of Granny's apartment. Tracy carried cans of water from the spigot and filled the holes Andrew dug. Then Granny set the tiny plants in the holes and surrounded them with dirt. Tracy worked quietly, thinking about Lisa. Granny's and Andrew's conversation drifted around her.

Her thoughts were interrupted when Doug called out the window. "I just phoned River City Hospital," he said. "Lisa's still unconscious, and just 'holding her own.' That's what Mrs. Curran said when she answered the telephone in her room."

Tracy and Doug exchanged worried glances. Was Lisa going to pull through? Would she ever be able to tell what she had seen in the jewelry store? Tracy shuddered as she refilled her can with water.

By lunch all the tomatoes were transplanted. Granny went inside to fix lunch while Andrew and Tracy finished the staking.

Andrew wiped his glistening forehead. "I'm sorry about this trouble with your mother," he said.

"It's good to see a family like yours stick together the way you do. I wish now that I'd married and raised a family." His tone was wistful.

"I can't imagine not having a family. It seems like a lonely way to live."

"It is lonely." He tied the last strip of cloth around the last tomato stake. "Well, guess I'll head home." He brushed off his hands.

At Granny's back door, Tracy paused with her hand on the doorknob. "Why don't you join us for lunch?" she asked. "I know Granny would like it. She always fixes enough food for an army." She smiled uncertainly.

Surprise flashed across Andrew's face. "Thanks, Tracy. I believe I will." After wiping his feet in the grass, he followed her up the back steps.

Although hungry, Tracy could barely swallow her sandwich. All she could think about was going to the farm alone again that afternoon. After lunch Tracy studied the darkening sky as she started down the street.

Turning the corner at Main Street, Tracy spotted Bert. He held a closed black umbrella and tapped the sidewalk with its shiny point. He waved at her when he was still half a block away.

Tracy remembered he was to help Granny put up screens that afternoon. "Hi, Bert," she called.

"I guess you finished cleaning up at the gym already."

"Yup," he agreed. "Hope to get your grandmother's chores done before it rains too." He peered up at the gloomy sky. "You should be carrying an umbrella yourself. Where are you off to?"

"Just to Granny's farm for a while."

Bert rubbed his jaw thoughtfully. "Why not take my umbrella? Or better yet, wait until the sun comes out to walk so far."

"Thanks, but I'll be okay," Tracy said, moving down the sidewalk. "There's something I need to take care of right away."

Tracy stared blindly in store windows downtown, her thoughts on Lisa. Had her accident really been an accident? Or could she have such valuable information that someone had tried to get rid of her? The confused questions whirled in Tracy's mind. Almost without realizing it, she had traveled the gravel road to the deserted farm.

While plodding up the driveway, a sudden gust of wind blew dirt into Tracy's eyes. Leaves overhead rustled. Faint thunder rolled in from the west. She decided to hunt quickly for her notebook and leave before the storm broke.

The shed door was still shut and barred, and Tracy decided to look there first. She searched first on the ground outside the shed, but found nothing. When she opened the door, light from the doorway fell on the worktable. In the middle of the table, next to some pruning shears, was her green notebook. Kicking the door open wide, Tracy dashed into the shed. She grabbed her notebook and was back outside before the door swung shut.

Tracy leaned against the rough boards of the shed and flipped through her notebook. As far as she could tell, no pages were missing. She put the notebook in her pocket, but something puzzled her. How could she have dropped the notebook so that it landed on the worktable? It didn't make sense.

Suddenly Tracy gasped. There was no way she could have lost the notebook at the farm Tuesday! She distinctly recalled making notes in it when she questioned Bert *Wednesday* night.

Now she knew! She must have lost her notebook in the scuffle with Mr. Whitaker. Or else he'd picked her pocket. How did she know he was really a private investigator anyway?

She frowned in confusion. If he had taken her notebook, how did it get in the shed? Had the mysterious "Mr. Gray" come to the farm that night? She had only his word for it that he was going back to River City.

Deep in thought, Tracy checked the house to make sure it was still locked. After trying both doors, she decided to take a quick walk by the other buildings.

Thunder rumbled louder, reminding Tracy of the impending storm. She hiked past the chicken house and the milk house. Everything looked exactly as it had earlier in the week. But striding past the barn, she halted and caught her breath sharply.

The overgrown grass and weeds had stood so straight last Tuesday. Now patches were matted down. Someone had been walking through the tall grass behind the barn recently, and more than once.

She bent down to examine the faint path. The moist skin on the back of her neck began to tingle. Tracy had an eerie feeling that she knew where the trail would lead if she followed it to its end.

Straightening, she zigzagged along the path of flattened grass. A vague fear filled her as she picked her way around rusty saws and an old plow. Halfway across the weedy patch behind the barn, she stopped. *Right about here*, she thought, turning slowly in a circle. She spotted a depression in the ground just ahead and inched toward it.

Weeds and grass had grown over the edges of the hole. Staring down into the dry well, the memories rushed back. Tracy's stomach lurched as she remembered the terrifying hours spent alone down there, afraid she was lost forever.

Squatting, Tracy peered into the blackness.

With the sky darkened, she could only see about five feet into the well. Three feet down, the missing ladder leaned against one side of the dirty well.

Lightning flashed, but Tracy remained motionless on the edge of the hole. She refused, for a few minutes, to even consider the next obvious step. If only she could leave it up to Doug. But with his cast, he couldn't investigate the well for her.

Tracy knew she should be thrilled that she'd probably just discovered the thief's hiding place. But her mind was blank—except for the sheer terror of going back down into that well.

10

The Clue in the Well

Clouds rolled in the west, bumping into each other and careening off. Thunder rumbling in the distance reminded Tracy that her time was short. She wanted to get back to Granny's before the storm broke.

Taking a deep breath and forcing it out between clenched teeth, she crept to the edge of the well. With her legs over the side, she tried to reach the ladder's top rung. Her legs were too short by several inches.

Tracy turned around and knelt at the edge of the well. Lying on her stomach, she wiggled backwards and dropped her legs into the hole. Her dangling feet groped for the ladder.

When her toes touched the top rung, she wriggled back until her full weight rested on the ladder. Peering down into the darkness, Tracy's knees wobbled. Gripping the ledge, she dropped one foot down to the next rung. On the third rung, her eyes reached ground level.

She continued—rung by rung—to the floor of the well. Looking up, Tracy saw the dim circle of daylight above her. She sensed the sides of the well closing in. Reaching out, she touched moisture on its rocky sides.

Kneeling on the hard earth at the bottom, she felt around on the ground. Her hands brushed over several small objects. Finally she found what felt like a flashlight. When she slid a button forward with her thumb, a dim circle of light shone on the gray stone wall. The flashlight revealed only a few square inches at a time. Still, Tracy felt relieved as the suffocating darkness was pushed back a little.

Pointing the wavering light down, Tracy squinted at several objects on a wooden box. A white paper lay on top. Excitedly, Tracy held the paper up close to the light and read.

"River City Pawn Shop" was typed across the top. Near the bottom was listed the date, three days earlier. Tracy squinted and read, "One diamond ring—large center stone plus four small stones." The price received for it was listed, but she couldn't make out the signature scrawled across the bottom of the paper.

Tracy whistled as she realized she held the pawn ticket for a ring probably stolen from Simms—and no doubt signed by the real thief! *At last* she had concrete proof of her mother's innocence!

Kneeling by the box, Tracy played the flashlight over several other objects. *There must be more evidence here somewhere.* She lifted a round flat object into the flashlight beam. Something stirred in her memory as she rubbed the ornate gold cover . . . .

In a flash, she was back in the alley by Simms, asking Bert Benson a question—then saw him check the time for her—on the gold watch she held in her hand.

Suddenly weak, Tracy leaned against the side of the well. Bert must be the thief! She could think of no other reason why his watch and a pawn ticket were hidden in the well.

Tracy inspected the rest of the floor. While she hunted, her mind leap-frogged from one memory to another. First, Bert had insisted that he never worked nights at Simms, but she'd spotted him there the night before. He could easily have been there other nights too. Bert must have also taken her notebook, Tracy realized. Was he afraid she had recorded too much in her notes?

Without wanting to, Tracy remembered Lisa Curran's terrified face as she searched the gym Friday night. Who had she been hunting for? Bert had been at the bazaar. Was Bert the hit-and-run driver?

Louder thunder interrupted her dizzying thoughts. Looking up, Tracy felt two drops of water hit her face. She knew she had to hurry, so she flashed the light around the well one last time. She glimpsed the corner of an envelope sticking out from under the wooden box.

She pulled out the envelope. When she removed the letter inside, a photograph fluttered to the cold floor. Retrieving the picture, Tracy held it in front of the feeble light and stared hard. Something hazy stirred in the back of her mind. The tall thin man in the yellowed picture looked familiar—something about the eyes and the mouth. But the picture had been taken a long time ago.

Unfolding the brittle letter, she began to read. Her eyes widened. At the end of the letter, she leaned weakly against the ladder. *Now* it finally made sense, including the signature on the pawn ticket.

A sudden picture of Bert twirling an umbrella flashed through Tracy's mind. She'd forgotten he was at Granny's. Stuffing the photograph and letter in her pocket, she grabbed for the ladder.

In her haste Tracy bumped against the wall and dropped the flashlight. There was only the sound of breaking glass before the light went out. Tracy stood frozen in the bottom of the old well, staring up into the darkening sky.

I can't be trapped down here again! Tracy screamed inwardly. *I have to get out of here!*

Taking deep shuddering breaths, she began groping for the ladder. In her terror, she'd almost forgotten that a criminal was in Granny's apartment at that very moment. And Granny's only protection was a boy with a broken leg.

When Tracy found the ladder, she gripped its sides and began to climb. With each step up, rain fell more heavily. Her hair was soon plastered to her head. Grasping each slippery rung, she climbed the last two steps.

Tracy flung herself over the edge of the well and landed in the soggy grass. Lightning flashed over her head as she dragged her legs out of the well.

Dark sheets of rain hung from gray clouds in the west. Tracy wished she had a jacket or umbrella. Then she remembered a sheet of plastic under the workbench. Dashing to the shed, she took shears and cut a hole in the center of the plastic. Slipping it over her head, the homemade poncho hung nearly to the ground.

Running down the gravel driveway, Tracy kept pulling the wet plastic away from her legs. But with each step, the poncho wrapped itself more tightly around her body. It seemed an eternity before she reached Main Street. By then the rain had nearly stopped. Tracy raced, unseeing, past Centerville's stores.

Half a block from Granny's apartment, Tracy spied Bert outside carrying a large screen. She hid behind a huge elm tree until he disappeared around the apartment toward the front of the building.

Granny stepped out of the kitchen door carrying a laundry basket. Tracy watched her remove dripping clothes from the clothesline, then carry the basket inside. Tracy knew she would hang the wet clothes on a makeshift clothesline strung across the kitchen.

She whipped out her notebook and pencil and flipped to an empty page. In a quick series of dots, she wrote:

Even if Doug didn't remember the entire Braille alphabet, he could make out her urgent message: BERT REAL THIEF.

Tracy ripped the message from her notebook and folded it twice. She crept toward the kitchen's back door, watching the corner of the building.

Slipping into the kitchen, she noted with relief that only Doug was there. He relaxed at the table, an open book propped against a bowl of apples, and glanced up as she closed the door.

"Shh-h-h-h." Tracy held a finger to her lips. Cocking her head, she overheard Granny talking to Andrew in the living room.

Tracy tiptoed across the kitchen to whisper in Doug's ear. Pulling aside the curtains, she saw Bert heading for the kitchen door. Without a word, she dropped the Braille note in Doug's lap.

Tracy ducked under Granny's makeshift clothesline, nearly tripping over a loose coil of clothesline on the floor. Hopping over it, she scooted down the hall and into Granny's bedroom.

With the door ajar, she heard Bert come into the kitchen. Tracy breathed deeply, trying to still her racing heart. Blood pounded so loudly in her head that it was difficult to hear.

Now that it was actually time to catch the thief, Tracy found her mind going totally blank. Panicky, she couldn't think of a single workable plan to trap Bert. She'd just have to play it by ear.

Her attention was caught as Granny called Bert and Andrew to the table. "I've set out some of my apricot bread," she said, "and I'll be mad if you leave even a crumb."

"No chance of that with me around, Granny!" Tracy was relieved to hear Doug's voice sound normal.

Feet shuffled in the kitchen. "Don't mind if I do" and "Looks good, Ella Mae" floated down the hallway to the bedroom. Tracy edged close to the half-open door and heard Bert's voice. "I ran into Tracy on the way here this afternoon," he said pleasantly. "She said she was on the way to your farm."

Tracy closed her eyes to listen better, concentrating on every word. Granny answered him. "Tracy and her mother both like to spend time out there. It's always been their favorite place."

"I just hope she doesn't catch pneumonia in this drenching rain," Bert said. "Do you know why she went out there?" To Tracy's alert ears, Bert sounded too eager for information.

"She left something there earlier this week," Doug said.

Granny laughed. "I just hope she doesn't get locked in the shed again." She paused and Tracy heard footsteps. "It's still stormy-looking outside. Now that you mention it, I wonder what's keeping her."

Now's my chance, Tracy thought. She stepped into the short hallway. Five steps later, she was in the kitchen.

"Here I am, Granny," she said, watching Bert. "I got back a little while ago." All four of them stared at her.

Granny's face lit up with surprise. "Tracy! I didn't hear you come in. What did you do at the farm?"

"I had a really interesting visit," Tracy said carefully. "You'll never guess, Granny. Remember that old well I fell down when I was little? I found it again today."

Without saying a word, Bert slowly wiped his mouth with a napkin. His piercing eyes never left Tracy's face.

Granny paused with her knife in the air. "What in the world were you doing behind the barn? I'd think falling down that well once would have been enough for you."

"I didn't fall in this time. Someone put a ladder in the well. I just climbed down."

Although Tracy watched Bert from the corner of her eye, she felt, rather than saw, him tense up. He seemed ready to pounce, like a caged tiger at the zoo.

"You climbed down in that dirty old well?" Granny shook her head. "Did you find anything?"

In the stillness of the kitchen, Tracy heard Bert's heavy breathing. "Yes, I found evidence of—"

Tracy broke off, whirling in time to see Bert spring from the edge of his chair. In one swift motion, he lunged toward her. The growl deep in his throat matched the sinister look on his face.

"Why, you sneaky little brat," he snarled, his arms outstretched. But before his hands reached her, Doug expertly swung his leg out. Bert saw him too late and tripped over his cast, crashing to the kitchen floor.

Granny shrieked. "Bert! Doug! What's going on?"

Bert and Doug ignored her. Bert's hands clutched toward Doug's throat as he half-rose from the floor. Tracy searched frantically for a weapon, and, spying Bert's umbrella by the door, she grabbed it and spun around. With the curved handle, Tracy hooked Bert's leg. Yanking with all her strength, Tracy knocked Bert off balance. He fell back heavily to the floor. Doug quickly pushed himself on top of him.

"Help, Granny!" Tracy yelled as she jumped on Bert's back too. "Bert's the real thief! Grab that piece of clothesline!"

Bert thrashed around angrily on the floor. But with Tracy sprawled across his legs and Doug flung across his back, he jerked only a few inches back and forth.

Granny grabbed the clothesline and quickly

bound Bert's ankles. With another piece, she tied his hands behind his back. Doug added the final touch with his red bandana. Gagging the cursing janitor, he secured the bandana firmly behind his head.

"Yea for Tracy!" Doug shouted from his perch on Bert's shoulders.

Granny leaned against the refrigerator, fanning her pale face with her apron. "Are you sure, Tracy?" asked her grandmother.

"There's no mistake," Tracy said grimly. "I found concrete evidence down in the well that Bert's our thief."

Granny collapsed into her chair. Andrew sat motionless, staring at his uneaten bread. He seemed to be in shock.

"I'll call the police in a minute, but tell us what you found," Doug said.

"First, I found that the farm was being used as a hiding place, just like we thought," Tracy said. "But I never suspected Bert was the one who had broken into the farmhouse. I believed everything Bert told us."

"Like what?" Doug asked.

"For one thing, he said he never worked nights at Simms, but last night on the way home I saw him in the back of the jewelry store. He had easy access to the safe," Tracy explained.

Doug nodded. "And Bert was at the bazaar. He could have overheard Lisa telling you she had information about the robbery." His eyes widened. "And on his way to the jewelry store, he could have hit Lisa."

Granny frowned, the color slowly coming back into her checks. "I'm afraid you may have made a mistake, Tracy. All you have is circumstantial evidence. Plus, you forget one thing. The police said the safe wasn't even broken into."

Tracy continued pacing around the table, playing with a piece of clothesline. "He didn't have to tamper with the safe," she said. "He had help from someone who had experience cracking safes."

Tracy stopped beside Andrew's chair and spoke to his bowed head. "If you promise not to go anywhere, we won't tie you up too."

Granny gasped. "Tracy! What on earth are you saying?"

Tracy looked from Granny's shocked face to Doug's. "I told you Bert had help. Meet his accomplice," Tracy answered. "This is Bert's Uncle Andrew."

11

Dreams

Doug's mouth hung open as he straddled Bert's back. Granny's face blanched to a pasty white and she gripped the sides of her chair.

"I'm afraid it's true," Tracy said. "Andrew is Bert's uncle. They worked together on the jewelry thefts. This isn't the first time either."

Bert chewed angrily on his gag and managed the garbled words, "Brat kids."

"How do you know this?" Granny demanded, her voice breaking.

Tracy reached into her pocket. She pulled out the musty-smelling letter she'd found in the well. Inside the envelope was the yellowed photograph. Tracy handed the picture to Granny first, who then passed it to Doug.

"Who's this?" Doug peered closer. "Wait a

minute. The younger man looks like Bert. Is the tall one Andrew?"

Tracy nodded. "According to the letter, that picture was taken nearly twenty years ago. By the way, 'Bert' is really Bernard Blackburn, the son of Andrew's brother. When Bernard was orphaned at age three, Andrew took him north to live with him."

Granny stared at Andrew. "Is this true?"

Andrew nodded miserably. "Yes, I raised him while I worked on the railroad." He stared at the clothesline rope coiled on the table.

Doug scratched his leg above the cast. "Tracy, you said that Simms wasn't the first jewelry theft. What are you talking about?"

"Maybe I should read you part of the letter." Tracy skimmed down the page. "It was written last year from Arizona just after Andrew moved into his apartment. Here's the place:

> If you're thinking of turning down my idea, think twice. I want out of the country. I have to get my hands on at least $10,000. If you don't help me crack some Centerville safes, I'll give the cops in Salem a little tip. I bet they'd still like to know who cracked the safe in that robbery. I served time, but I kept my mouth shut

116

about you, Uncle. You got off free, thanks to me. Now you owe me. Help me once more, then I'll vanish without a trace.''

Doug frowned. "They robbed a store in Salem?"

Tracy nodded. "The police will have no trouble tracking down the robbery. Bert served time for it, so he has a record. Since he wants to leave the country, he's no doubt wanted by the police for more recent crimes.''

Granny touched the older man's shoulder. "But, why, Andrew? Why did you do it?"

The silence was thick in the tiny kitchen. Finally Andrew spoke. "I don't expect you to understand, Ella Mae." He rubbed his balding head with a trembling hand. "I never had enough to eat when I was a kid. I dropped out of school in the fourth grade to go to work. Later I went north to work on the railroad where the pay was better." His voice was so low that Tracy had to move closer to hear.

"Then what happened?" Granny asked quietly.

"There was never enough money, especially after Bernie came to live with me. There were so many things he needed, and I wanted to give them to him. When I got laid off the railroad, I worked odd jobs, but it wasn't nearly enough. Bernie was in trouble a lot, and when he was older, we robbed a jewelry store. I wasn't caught." Andrew's head sagged forward on his chest. His confession seemed to have exhausted him.

Bert managed to spit out his soggy gag. "Cut the sob story, Uncle! You're as much to blame as I was."

"Dry up, you." Doug stuffed the gag back into Bert's mouth.

Tracy sank into the chair opposite Andrew. "So when Bert showed up in Centerville, he became the janitor. He blackmailed you into helping him with more jewelry thefts, right?" Tracy slowly crumbled the remains of Doug's apricot bread.

Andrew nodded, but didn't lift his head.

Doug shook his head in disbelief. "Did you find the missing jewelry in the well? Can we prove they stole it?"

"No, but I found a ticket from a River City pawn shop," Tracy said, pulling the ticket from her pocket. "It says that last week a diamond ring was pawned, and its description is given. It took me a while to see that the signature on the ticket was Andrew's."

"If the ring is still at the pawn shop, that should be enough," Doug said. "But I wonder where the rest of the jewelry is?"

In answer to his question, Tracy moved the

bread from the table, then she spread out an old newspaper. After bringing three of Granny's plants to the kitchen, she dumped the red-orange geraniums and the philodendron out of their pots onto the newspaper. Pebbles from the bottom of the pots were mixed in with the dirt.

Tracy poked through the soil. Nodding, she brushed the dirt from three small plastic bags, then showed them to Granny and Doug. Through the dirty plastic, they saw two shining rings and one gold necklace.

"I'm sorry, Granny," Tracy said. "When Andrew repotted these plants this week, he also hid the stolen jewelry in the dirt."

Granny fingered the dirty bags. "Then you were pretending to be my friend just to hide the jewelry in my house?"

Andrew remained slumped over in his chair, silent.

Tracy almost wished Granny sounded angry, but she only seemed very hurt. "Probably he was friendly with us because Mom worked at Simms. He found out a lot about the store from Mom, just by acting interested. And, of course, Bert got a job there as janitor. It worked out perfectly."

Andrew cleared his throat. His bloodshot eyes looked sunken in his wrinkled face. "I know it won't help, Ella Mae, but I *am* sorry. I admit I was friendly with you so I could find out about Simms from your daughter. At first, that is. After a while, I enjoyed being here, getting to know your family. I hated it when Laura was arrested. I hadn't counted on that, but by then it was too late."

For a full two minutes, nothing was said. Granny painstakingly repotted her plants, seeming totally absorbed in her task. Then wiping her dirty hands on her apron, she turned. "I'm sorry how things turned out, Andrew. But I think I understand—at least a little."

Tracy's stomach churned at the mixture of feelings inside her. Finding out about Andrew had been a shock. She honestly believed he'd been an unwilling participant in the robberies.

But most of Tracy's thoughts were about her mother. She would never go to trial, and everyone would know she was innocent. It was all over.

Tracy moved to the telephone in the hallway. Slowly she dialed the number of the Centerville Police Station.

Tracy leaned back on her elbows on the dusty floor of the farmhouse living room. Granny, Doug, Tracy, and her mother had brought their Sunday dinner out to the farm. The huge old wicker picnic basket sat open in the middle of the floor.

Tracy could hardly believe that it was all over.

Andrew and Bert were in jail, and her mother was home for good. Even so, Tracy still had some unanswered questions.

She leaned over and scribbled a tic-tac-toe on her brother's cast. "Doug, did you ever suspect Andrew?" she asked.

"No, I always trusted Andy. In fact, I discussed Mom's case with him many times. I guess those walks he took me on were just to pump me for information."

"Don't feel that way, Doug," Granny said sternly. "That may have been his intention at first. But I truly believe he enjoyed our family after he got to know us. I think he got caught up in something he couldn't stop."

"A lot of clues happened right under my nose," Tracy said, changing the subject. "One evening uptown I saw Andrew get on the bus to River City. He *said* he was going to the city library, but it was pretty late. That was the night he pawned the ring for Bert."

"What else?" Granny asked, folding her hands.

Tracy hesitated. "Well, I did wonder why he kept repotting your plants so often. But like Doug, I assumed it was just an excuse to see you."

"I guess we know that's not true anymore," Granny said, a catch in her voice.

Tracy hurried on. "Once at the library I saw

Andrew reading the society page of the newspaper. The announcement was about Mr. and Mrs. Simms's anniversary party. The paper gave the date of their wedding twenty years ago.''

"So?" Doug looked puzzled.

"I recalled reading that people often use important personal dates as combinations to their safes. You know, dates of births and anniversaries. They're easy to remember.'' Tracy pulled her notebook and pencil from her pocket to demonstrate. "Mr. Simms used the date of his birthday as the combination to the downstairs safe. He used the date of their anniversary—the date from the paper—as the combination to a small wall safe in his office upstairs. They were married April 26, 1966. So the combination was 4–26–66. Andrew was reading about the Simms family to try to discover some of these dates.''

Doug snapped his fingers. "I remember once when he asked me about Bryan Simms. He asked the date of his birthday when I did the magic show at his party.''

"That would be one of the dates he passed along to Bert. They tried various dates to see if they could open the safe easily. Of course that's the reason the safe didn't look broken into.''

Their mother reached into the picnic basket for another piece of chicken. "Don't feel badly that you didn't spot him as a thief. Weeks before the first robbery, I gave him some information myself. *I* was the one who told Andrew the date of Mr. Simms's birthday. I'd made a cake. The day Granny decorated it for me, Andrew was there and asked lots of questions.''

"By the way, how did Andrew and Bert know about the old well?" Tracy asked. "Did you tell them, Granny?"

Granny shook her head.

"I did," Doug said sheepishly. "The day you were trapped in the shed, Andrew came over. I told him why you were so afraid of small dark places. I told him about when you fell into that dry well."

"That's okay," Tracy said. "I guess we were all taken in by Bert and Andrew. Personally, I think Bert is the real crook. I don't think Andrew even wanted to be a part of the robberies."

Tracy's mother nodded. "He certainly would have no part of hurting someone—like the hit-and-run accident."

Granny's face brightened. "How could I have forgotten! This morning I called the River City Hospital. Lisa's conscious and feeling much better. It looks like she'll be all right."

"That's great!" Tracy licked the brownie frosting from her fingers. "I still wonder what she wanted to tell me."

"I asked the police," Granny said. "She told them that late one night she'd seen Bert in the jewelry store, searching Mr. Simms's desk. He probably overheard her speak to you at the bazaar. The police said Bert denies being the hit-and-run driver. In all fairness, it could have been someone else."

"The important thing is that Lisa will be all right," Tracy's mother said. "I'd like to go to the hospital tomorrow and take some flowers. I want her to know how much I appreciate her effort to help me. But right now, I'm going to clean up this mess. Picnic or not, we don't want our living room overrun with ants."

"Now that everything's cleared up, will you go back to work at Simms?" Doug asked.

"Yes, I think so. There aren't that many jobs in Centerville. I hope to keep working there, even if he sells the store. And I plan to work twice as hard remodeling out here so we can move soon."

"I can't wait." Doug surveyed the room. "We'll spread sleeping bags in this room near the stove, and carry clean water up from the creek, and—"

His mother laughed. "We won't have to be quite *that* primitive. But I think we should definitely plan to move by the end of the summer."

Tracy grinned at their enthusiasm. Her mother

saw the smile and shrugged. "I know you think this is a crazy dream, Tracy. But we'll find the money somehow."

"I wasn't going to say it's crazy. In fact, I think with the four of us working hard this summer, we could get a lot done."

Doug raised one eyebrow. "You're always the one who says to 'be practical.' What's up?"

"Well, I *still* think you have to be patient and work hard. But without dreaming first, you really don't have a goal, or something to work for." She reached into her pocket, pulled out a folded piece of paper, and handed it to her mother. "I know this won't pay for much, but it's a start."

"Where did you get this check?" her mother asked.

"It's a reward from Mr. Simms for catching the real jewel thieves. He called early this morning and asked me to come down to the store. He was really embarrassed when I got there. He gave me the money then." Grinning, she rocked back and forth on her heels. "I also walked by Kids Korner on my way home. Mrs. Jenkins was out front, and she offered me a job for the summer. A *paying* job!"

Her mother grabbed her hand and pulled her close. "That's wonderful! I know how much you love working there."

Tracy examined the rough, cracked plaster

walls of the living room. "If we pool our money, we can fix up quite a few things this summer. We can work most evenings and weekends." Tracy noticed her mother's surprised face. "I know this reward money and the money from our summer jobs won't pay for everything, but it's a beginning. After we move in, we can work in stages, fixing up one room at a time."

Her mother strode briskly around the echoing room. "It will be a lot of hard work," she warned, "but I know we can do it!"

Doug draped an arm over his sister's shoulders. "If money's a problem, I know where Tracy can make some. She can get an office downtown and hire out as a private detective. I'd even buy her a new notebook."

Tracy threw a chicken bone at him. She knew he was joking, but she didn't intend to do any detecting again for a long time.